The Sons of Rissouli

A Danny Lansing Adventure

www.stridentpublishing.co.uk

STRIDENT

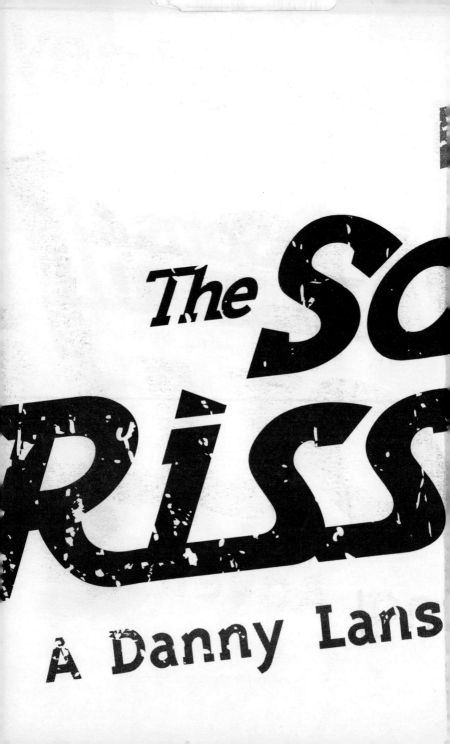

The So

Riss

A Danny Lans

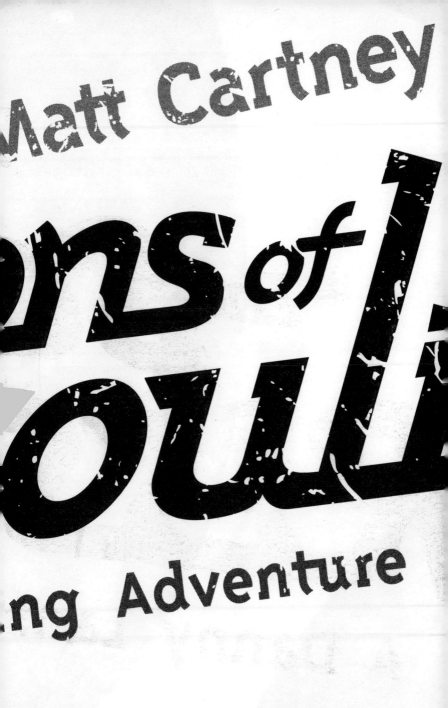

Matt Cartney

ns of oul

ng Adventure

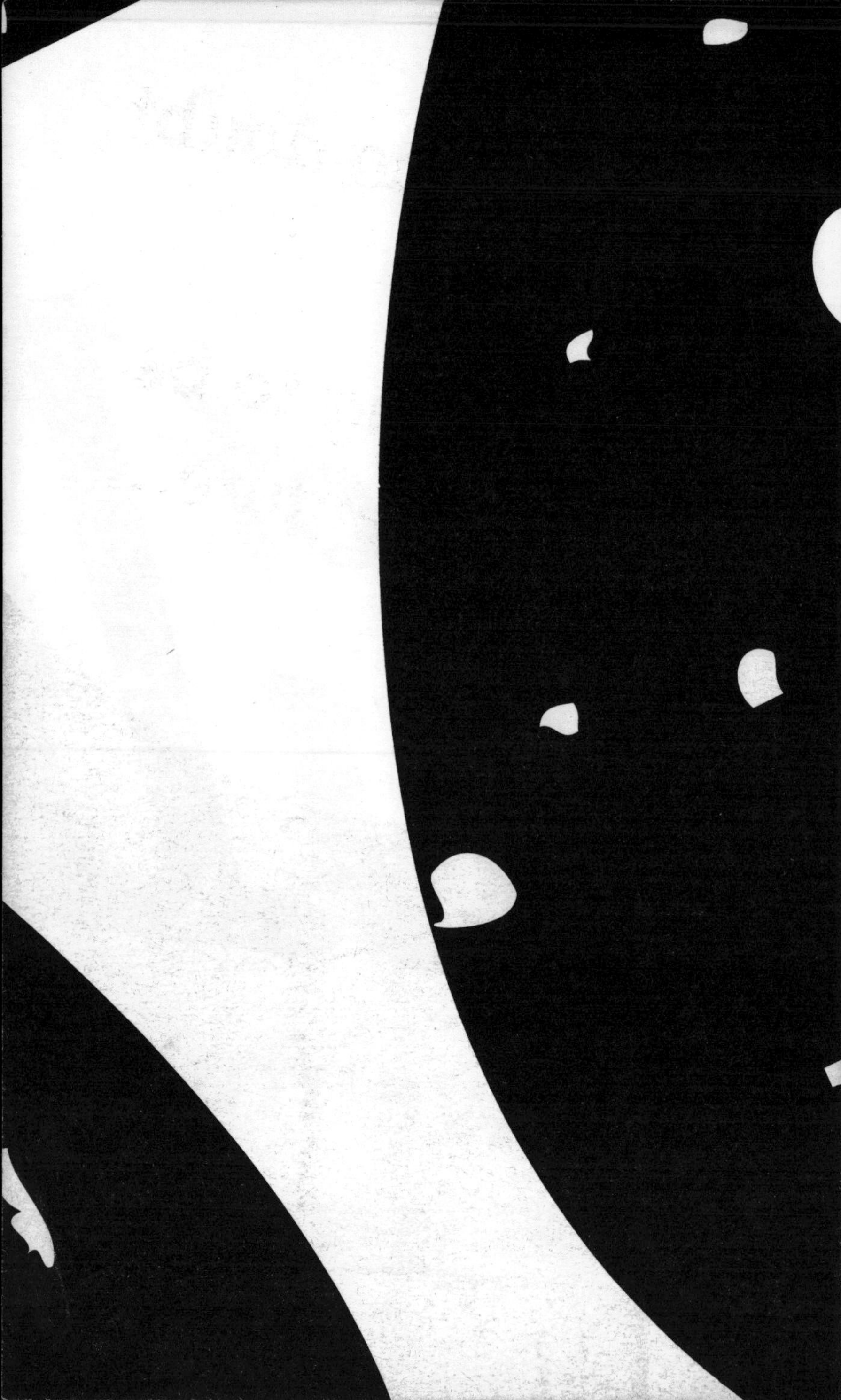

There's no doubt about it.

It's going to be an adventure...

Published by
Strident Publishing Ltd
22 Strathwhillan Drive
The Orchard, Hairmyres
East Kilbride G75 8GT

Tel: +44 (0)1355 220588
info@stridentpublishing.co.uk
www.stridentpublishing.co.uk

A catalogue record for this book is
available from the British Library.

978-1-905537-21-1

The publisher acknowledges subsidy from the
Scottish Arts Council towards the publication of this volume.

Typeset in Bembo by Lawrence Mann
Cover image © Lawrence Mann.co.uk 2011
Printed by CPI Cox & Wyman

FOR
MUM AND DAD

MATT CARTNEY

When he's not working and writing, Matt Cartney is an intrepid traveller, mountaineer and snow-boarder. His love of adventure is infectious; presenting in schools, bookshops and libraries he includes photographs and stories of his exploits from around the world. He is always willing to try new things, whether it is cycle touring in Australia, skiing across a Norwegian mountain range or attempting to ride his motorcycle to Nepal (an attempt cut short by terrorists in Baluchistan).

Matt lives in Edinburgh. *The Sons of Rissouli* is the first novel in the Danny Lansing series. If you would like him to do a presentation at your school, you can email him on mc.photojournalism@gmail.com

PROLOGUE

Danny Lansing woke with a start. Shifting uncomfortably in his seat, he remembered where he was and why he was there.

His chest suddenly welled with the pain of the memory and he screwed his eyes shut in an attempt to retreat back into the oblivion of sleep, willing the droning of the engine and the rolling of the cab to help him slip back into unconsciousness. It was no good though; try as he might he kept thinking about his mum and dad. Seeing them around the kitchen table or in the garden, remembering their funny comments and mannerisms, how they were always laughing and talking. Full of life.

He peered through the darkness at his Uncle Angus, crouched low in the driving seat of his old pick-up truck, his collar turned up against the cold. His face, dimly lit by the orange glow thrown up from the speedometer, looked creased and drawn, like a gargoyle with depression. Danny felt he had lost him too, because this was not the man he had once known.

★ ★ ★

Uncle Angus was his mother's much younger brother who used to visit them in Cumbria. On an evening early in the summer, Danny would hear the throaty growl of Angus's huge off-road motorbike as it wound its way up the hillside roads. Even at a distance it sounded stronger, yet heavier and lazier, than the ordinary sports bikes that normally whined up and down past the house, startling the cat and irritating his mother.

Angus always looked tanned, was always grinning and had always just been somewhere unbelievably cool: Alaska, Iran, Botswana, Borneo – exotic, strange and exciting places. And he had no shortage of stories to tell: stories about wild lands, dangerous enemies and the finest of friends. Of close shaves that made Dad laugh and Mum purse her lips and drum the tabletop with her fingers. Of the sights, sounds and smells of adventures that Danny would have given everything to have been a part of.

He wanted more than anything to do the things that Angus did, to go where he had been, to get into the same scrapes and wing his way out of them with the same combination of brass-necked cheek, lunatic courage and pure dumb luck.

For about a week, Danny and Angus would spend their time blasting around the country lanes on Angus's motorbike, stopping to fish for trout, swim in rivers, and camp. Proper camping that is, with fires and rope swings and running around the woods till dawn. Sometimes it seemed to Danny that Angus enjoyed kid's stuff more than he did. Perhaps it was some kind of release. After being shot at (which seemed to happen to Angus on an almost monthly basis), charged by wild animals (at least once a year) and getting lost in the jungle/desert/

mountains (practically every week), jumping thirty feet off a bridge into a river must have been his equivalent to lying on the couch watching cartoons.

All too soon the week would be up for another year and off Angus would go, disappearing to who-knows-where until the following summer when Danny would hear that throaty rumble echo again through the Cumbrian hills.

Not any more though. Danny's home was now in Perthshire, with that self-same Uncle Angus. An Uncle Angus who had been silent and grim-faced for weeks.

They were heading there now in a rattling old pick-up with a broken heater. Through the window, Danny could see the dark shapes of rounded hills. On their summits were silver caps of snow that glistened under the star-spattered blackness of the night. There were no yellow squares of windows in the darkness, no sign of warmth or humanity at all. He stretched and yawned. 'Where are we?'

Angus stirred, then looked around and smiled. It was a weak effort but a smile nonetheless. 'We've just crossed the border. Another couple of hours and we'll be in Dunkeld.'

'That's where your house is?'

'Um… Yes.' Angus looked as though he was about to say something more, but decided against it and retreated back into his collar.

There was silence for a while and Danny stared out of the side window. Every now and then the glare of headlights would blot out the darkness and fill the night with a white light that made it impossible to see anything but the tiny crystal droplets in the misty glass in front of his nose. Slowly Danny's night vision returned and the myriad dark points of trees on hilltops stood out against the stars. Soon his eyelids felt heavy again and he decided not to ask Angus any more questions. It didn't seem the right time just now. But the problem was that it never seemed like the right time. He slipped back into a restless doze that lasted all the way to Dunkeld.

CHAPTER ONE

SIXTEEN MONTHS LATER

Angus ran his fingers through his coal-black hair and blew his cheeks out contemplatively. He was sitting at his ancient mahogany desk, staring out the window. His farmhouse and its outbuildings formed three sides of a square around a concrete yard. In one corner stood his battered Toyota pick-up and in another, a pile of timber, bricks and sand. The building materials had been there since he bought the house a few years ago and he had decided to leave them where they were until he found a use for them. He had a feeling that he would need to fix some terrible defect in this old house, but nothing had fallen down yet, so the pile stayed where it was.

Danny, however, had clearly decided what the stuff was for; it was for building a great wobbly ramp for him and his mates' bikes. Every time they went off it and landed without actually breaking anything (on either their bikes or themselves) they egged each other on to prop it higher with one more brick. It was clearly going to end in tears - and soon.

Angus knew that a *responsible* adult would have rushed out approximately three bricks ago and, after administering thick ears all round, sent everyone home with a stern lecture on health and safety. But Angus had never claimed to be a responsible adult. And besides, the kid and his mates were having too much fun. He was even tempted to have a go himself.

Despite being too young, obviously irresponsible and having no clue about bringing up children, Angus felt he was doing a pretty good job with the boy. Although, to be fair, Danny was largely bringing himself up. He was a good kid and Angus knew that given their respective pasts he was more likely to get *himself* into trouble than the boy was.

The only problem was his job. Angus was an investigative journalist and was good at it, at least the investigative part. He had a nose for a great story and knew by instinct when something didn't smell right. He had broken some of the biggest stories of the last few years; shattering a slave-trading organization in Eastern Europe, exposing corruption at the highest levels of a Middle Eastern oil company, and embarrassing some important gentlemen in Moscow so much that he would not risk returning to Russia for thirty or forty years.

Writing it all down afterwards was the only chore. He was a journalist not because he liked writing, but because he loved seeing exotic countries, experiencing other cultures, and the feeling that he was really living his life. Even more than that, he loved bringing down the bad guys. Bad guys with lots of money and power who thought they were untouchable were his favourites.

When this way of life was your bread and butter, becoming the legal guardian of a boy Danny's age was inconvenient to say the least. Angus could no longer simply throw a change of clothes, a camera and his laptop into a bag and head off into the unknown at a moment's notice. Danny was a smart kid but even

Angus realised he couldn't leave him to fend for himself while he travelled the world on the hunt for a big story.

The good news was that Danny's summer holidays were coming up soon. If Angus could break a suitably big story that he could sell for a decent amount of money, in a place with a beach or some other child-friendly distractions, maybe Danny would not mind going abroad for a while. Something like a diamond smuggling operation working out of a theme park would be ideal. Unfortunately, smuggling operations were famously thin on the ground in the immediate surroundings of theme parks.

'Oh well, I'll just have to see what I can turn up,' he said to himself. As he did, the phone rang. Picking it up, he heard someone clearing their throat at the other end. He recognised the peculiar wheezing cough immediately. 'Newby! How are things in the big smoke?'

'Angus? Is that you my lad? Great, lovely. How am I? You know, same old same old. When a man is tired of London he is tired of life and all that.' Chief Inspector Newby's clipped Etonian voice dropped to a conspiratorial whisper: 'I'm glad I caught you, there's something I'd like to talk to you about.'

'Really? That is good news. I'm going stir-crazy here. A bit of Newby-brand adventure is just what the doctor ordered.'

'Yes, well don't get too excited. It's all a bit vague and coincidental. There's more than a whiff of the hush-hush about it, too.'

'Hush-hush? I haven't heard that term since I saw a film about the Second World War.'

Newby sounded a little huffed, 'Don't mock lad. I'm from a generation for whom 'hush-hush' was deadly serious. If you are going to be like that, I'll keep my little nugget of info to myself...'

Angus laughed, he knew Newby wasn't serious. 'Sorry mate, go ahead. I promise not to take the mick out of your old school lingo.'

'Right then.' There was a brief pause and the sound of shuffling papers at the other end. 'I'll start at the beginning, shall I, best place no doubt? Do you remember about eighteen months ago the gangland murder of the teenager Gareth Desray? It was a huge story at the time. Desray was an A-grade student in an area so rough the pit-bulls go about in pairs. Shot in the head for some imagined disrespect of the local crack dealer. The gun used was a Brunton 9mm automatic.'

'Yes, I do. I thought you guys caught the perpetrator and put him away for a long stretch?' Angus interjected.

'We did. That's not what I'm getting at. Let me finish will you, old chap? Six months after that a Yardie gang boss was pulled over for speeding. Of course the opportunity to search his vehicle was taken. Lo and behold: several thousand bootleg DVDs, some stolen mobile phones, a great big bag of drugs – and a Brunton 9mm automatic.'

'A finger in many pies it would seem,' said Angus. It was all quite run-of-the-mill so far.

'Then, two months ago,' Newby continued, 'an unidentified body was found floating in the Thames. He had been shot twice and then finished off with a knife. The first bullet had done little more than part his hair in an unfashionable manner and then whizzed off to God knows where. The second hit him in the leg where it lodged in his thigh bone. Now this is where it gets interesting. Our forensics chaps removed that bullet and identified the gun that fired it as, yes you guessed it, a Brunton 9mm automatic.'

Newby paused to let this sink in. Angus could picture him easing back in his moth-eaten chair in New Scotland Yard with a self-satisfied grin, waiting eagerly for Angus to reply along the lines of: 'Cor Blimey! A Brunton 9mm! What a corker!'

Unfortunately Angus ruined the moment by saying, 'That's grand, Newby. What is particularly special about the Brunton 9mm?'

'Don't know much about guns, do you Angus?' muttered an exasperated Newby.

'No,' he replied emphatically. 'I try to avoid them at all costs. I've had way too many of them pointed at me by men with entirely justified grudges against me.'

'What makes this coincidence special, Angus, is that Brunton Armaments is a British company based in Hereford and only makes guns for the military. You cannot buy Brunton hardware anywhere in the world *unless* you are the representative of an approved government.'

Angus had to admit that this was interesting. How were thugs and criminals getting their hands on military hardware? Did their access stop at handguns or could they get hold of other stuff? Angus exhaled noisily as he imagined gang members running amok with machine guns, grenades and rocket launchers.

'So far, so promising,' he said. 'But what is so 'hush-hush' about all this? Isn't it just a straightforward case of light-fingered squaddies selling stolen weapons to the highest bidder? Embarrassing perhaps, but it hardly needs to be kept top-secret.'

'Well, hang on a minute.'

Angus could hear the creak of a chair, followed by a click. The scratchy clatter and whistle of Mozart being played on a cheap radio echoed in the background as Newby returned to the phone. 'Right, now we can talk freely.'

Angus laughed to himself. Newby could be ridiculously melodramatic.

'Special Branch thought it might be thieving squaddies too and investigated accordingly. But it seems the British Army doesn't buy Brunton hardware. Not so much as a stick with a nail in the end has ever been sold by Brunton to Her Majesty's Armed Forces, so these British-made guns must have come from a foreign source. Someone is smuggling them back into the country and selling them to drug dealers.' He paused for a moment. 'Anyway, this is where it all gets a bit mysterious. I personally spoke to our glorious leader, Sir Henry Carrick-Thompson, Head of Special Branch, KCB, QPM, about taking this investigation further, but he just went red in the face and muttered something about 'lack of resources' and 'concentrating on the war on terror' and assigned me to another case.'

'That's a bit odd,' said Angus. 'You'd think smuggling military hardware into the country would be a fairly pressing issue.'

'You would have thought so, wouldn't you? No, something about this is distinctly fishy. All the more so because I happen to know that not only did Carrick-Thompson and Lord Thomas Brunton, the owner of Brunton Armaments, spend their formative years together at Harrow, but they are both on the board of directors of Threadneedle Private Bank and both spend their Sundays at the Royal Blackheath Golf Club. It all reeks a bit too much of old boys watching each others' backs.'

'You don't seem to have much faith in your glorious leader.'

'Just because a chap has more gongs than a Chinese antique shop doesn't mean he's as pure as the driven. Oh, I don't suppose he's directly involved in anything illegal, but his reluctance to have even the briefest look at this case rings alarm bells for me.'

Angus stretched in his chair and thought about what he had been told. His sixth sense for these things told him this was a story, possibly a big one. Not exactly a diamond smuggling operation, but he reckoned it was worth a look. He would pop down to London for a week or so. Danny should be able to amuse himself in the capital, giving Angus the opportunity to see if there really was something in all this.

'Right,' Angus said decisively, 'I'm coming down to take a closer look, see you soon.' And with that, he tossed down the receiver.

At this moment a mop of dark ginger hair appeared round the door, followed by a slightly apprehensive face. 'Er, Angus…' There was a pregnant pause as Danny looked at his feet with embarrassment.

'Come on. Spit it out.'

'Er, I think Colin's broken his finger falling off his bike.'

'Really? Which one?'

Danny hesitated. It wasn't the reaction he had been expecting. 'The BMX.'

'I meant which finger.'

'Er, the pinky on his right hand.'

'There is some sticky tape under the sink,' said Angus with a grin. 'Tape it to the finger next to it and we'll take him down the hospital.'

'Oh right, OK then.' Danny disappeared again and shortly a clunking, rummaging sound could be heard coming from the kitchen. Angus smiled to himself. Yes, he was a good kid. He might even make himself useful one of these days.

★ ★ ★

It was a surprisingly fresh, misty morning in St. James's Park, the week before the schools broke up for the summer. Angus had engineered Danny's absence by sending a note to the head teacher saying: 'Unfortunately, Danny has contracted Dengue fever. This means he has to be quarantined at home until he is no longer a risk to the general public.'

He had asked Danny if he thought he should back it up with a forged instruction of quarantine from the Surgeon General. Danny had just rolled his eyes and replied that he was likely to be expelled for such flagrant lies. Only the fact that his head teacher was a half-wit meant they might get away with it.

It was 7 am and they were waiting on a cold bench for Newby to make his way down from his office in New Scotland Yard. Danny had refused Angus's offer of some cash to amuse himself in town; this sounded far more interesting.

Suddenly Danny was aware of a presence at his side and looked up to see a man standing there, with a lazy smile on his large oval face. Danny was amazed that such a substantial man could approach without them noticing.

'Hello, Newby,' greeted Angus cheerfully. 'A bit 'cold war' all this isn't it? Meeting in parks in the morning mist? I'm surprised we haven't got identical briefcases to swap.'

Newby chuckled and as he did so his wide shoulders bounced up and down in great lurches like an earthquake in a mountain range. Everything about him was large, from his twisted broken nose to his policeman's feet. He might be nearly sixty years old, but he was still an imposing figure. His unbelted, tan raincoat reached almost to his ankles and made him look like a pillar of sandstone, holding up the grand edifice of British Democracy.

'Hello old boy, keeping out of trouble I hope? Who's this young chap?'

Angus looked across at Danny. 'This..?' there was a brief reflective pause. 'He's my assistant.'

'Really?' returned Danny. 'I thought you were mine!'

Newby let out a loud guffaw and winked at Angus. 'Well he's clearly got more than a drop of the McKinlay family blood pumping in his veins!' Turning to Danny he thrust out a meaty hand. 'You must be Danny. It's good to meet you.

I've heard a lot about you from your uncle here.'

'All good, I hope?' Danny liked this old copper, he had a manner that put him immediately at ease.

'Well, all *interesting*, shall we say!' replied Newby, chuckling tectonically again. He looked at the sky and cleared his throat noisily. 'Now, I've brought you here, rather than my office, because while none of this is strictly secret, I get the impression Carrick-Thompson wouldn't greatly appreciate me gabbing to the press about it.'

'Then why tell us about it at all, if it might get you into trouble?' asked Danny, reddening as he realised that, as an assistant, he should probably keep his mouth shut and not ask stupid questions.

'Because, my lad, I hate to see criminals getting away with it,' replied Newby, not seeming to mind the interruption. 'Something about this whole thing stinks and if I had my way I'd put a team of coppers on it till we found what was producing the reek. Unfortunately my boss disagrees, so I have come to the best investigator I know outside of Scotland Yard.'

Impatient to get to the point, Angus cut in: 'Can you give us something to work on? I could do with the autopsy report on the Thames floater for a start. Case notes for the Desray shooting, obviously, and anything you have on the Yardie gang boss you arrested for speeding.'

'Way ahead of you, old chap,' declared Newby, patting his bulging briefcase. 'Now let's find a nice warm café.'

They spread the files out on a formica-topped table in an eatery on Victoria Street. It had condensation and small ads on the windows and cheerful waitresses with pretty smiles.

'Nothing like a fry-up while you're upholding the law!' said Newby as they tucked into a selection of chips, bread and meat of indeterminate origin, deep-fried and smothered in tomato sauce. It was fantastic.

Among the mass of typed papers were some large photographic prints. Newby shuffled these out and put them face down next to his elbow, before pushing the pile towards Angus.

'Here are the reports on the three cases relevant to your gun-running investigation. They are synopses but they contain all the most important information. The difficulty is that the guns are untraceable. The two we found had their serial numbers filed off making it impossible to tell which shipment they came from. If we knew that we would know where they were being smuggled from. As it is, the guns could be coming from any one of the twenty-seven countries that Brunton sell weapons to. You will need to find a common link between the three cases. Of course, both the man who shot Desray and the gang boss were drug dealers, so I'd look at the drugs angle first.'

'That's what I was thinking,' answered Angus. 'What are those pictures?'

'Er...' Newby glanced at Danny. 'The autopsy photos of the body pulled from the Thames. Probably not PG rated, if you know what I mean?'

Danny felt irritated that they thought he was too much of a child to see pictures of a dead body. On the other hand, he wasn't exactly desperate to see them. 'It doesn't matter,

I need a pee anyway,' he said and got up to leave them to it.

Newby passed them over to Angus. They showed a bloated corpse that was a milky-grey colour and wrinkled like a fingertip that's spent too long in the bath. A dark slit in the middle of his chest told the story of the last moments of the man's life.

With the various photos of the body was one of the dagger that had been used to finish the man off. It had a worn, chipped blade, darkened and stained by many years of use. The handle was of a curious design, carved from a dark wood and decorated with intricate silver patterns.

'Why didn't the killer take this with him? It looks antique, possibly valuable.'

'Yes, I wondered about that. The coroner's report says the dagger was pushed in with such force that the blade jammed solid between two ribs. Apparently it took the coroner some time and a great deal of effort to pull the thing out!' Newby grimaced. 'I expect when you've just stabbed some chap in the chest you don't hang around to retrieve the family cutlery. The coppers might show up and catch you… ha ha… red handed!'

At this moment, Danny appeared, drying his hands on the seat of his trousers.

'Here we go, Danny,' Angus placed the photo of the dagger down on the table between an empty coffee cup and a greasy, dimpled vinegar bottle. 'Your job is to see what you can find out about this. An online search might be a good starting point. Meanwhile I'm going to visit an old, um…

friend and see what I can dig up about the drugs that were being dealt by these two.'

★ ★ ★

The internet did not throw much light on it; all Danny could find out was that, from the shape of the handle, the dagger might be Moroccan. What he needed was the advice of an expert in North African and Western Saharan arts. So, in the late summer afternoon, Danny found himself standing nervously outside the School of Oriental and African Studies in Thornhaugh Street. He could not very well present some academic with the photo and claim to be a journalist following up a hot lead on international gun-running and murder; they would laugh in his face. However, while he needed a more plausible story than the truth, he hadn't been able to think of anything. He decided to do as Uncle Angus would have done; he'd wing it. He would simply go in and see where the situation took him. If they kicked him back out on the street he would find himself another expert on North African and Western Saharan arts. This being London, he thought, there ought to be one on pretty much every street corner.

Taking a deep breath, he shoved open the door and strode purposefully over to the reception desk. A bored-looking young woman with a dark ponytail belatedly noticed him and came to life. Sitting upright she flashed him a professional smile. 'Hello there, what can I do for you?'

'Good afternoon,' said Danny in his best polite voice.

'I wondered if it would be possible to see Professor Moon?'

'Er, do you have an appointment, sweetheart?' the receptionist asked a little uncertainly.

'No... it's a private matter.'

'Right. Um... I'll...' Picking up the phone she stabbed in a five digit number and after a brief pause said into the receiver, 'Professor Moon? There's a boy here to see you, says it's a private matter.' Another pause. 'No, I've never seen him before... Ginger. A bit unkempt.' She smiled at Danny as she said this to let him know it wasn't a criticism. 'Right, I'll send him up.' Danny grinned.

Professor Moon's office was a tiny box-room with grubby windows that had been painted shut some time in the 1970s, sealing in a filing system favoured by eccentric academics the world over: the multiple-chaotic-mounds-of-paper-system.

Professor Moon eyed Danny quizzically over the top of her steel-framed spectacles. 'What is it young man, how can I help you?'

'Hi, I'm really sorry to trouble you, this won't take a minute. It's just I've hit a dead end and I didn't know where else to go.'

'I see. Well, let me have it then, I'm quite busy.' She was looking at him with a mixture of curiosity and impatience. Danny realised he would have to say something. Experience had taught him impatience often ended conversations prematurely with adults. Often before he had got round to the nitty-gritty of gouging them for pocket money/unhealthy snacks/a lift to the skate-park. He took a deep breath.

'My great-grand-dad is ninety next week.'

There was a long pause as Danny tried to work out how this could possibly be relevant to a carved dagger found sticking out of the chest of a dead guy who'd been fished out of the Thames.

'Oh that's nice.' Luckily by now she was starting to smile. Danny's natural talent for charming middle-aged ladies was working. As he realised he might actually be in with a chance of getting the information he needed, his brain went into overdrive, and his story clicked into place like the well-oiled parts of a precision instrument.

'Yeah, he's ninety, and I'm doing a project on his life. As a sort of birthday present, if you see what I mean. It's all been quite simple so far. I, well that is to say, my older brother and me, got lots of info about his old school, from the regiment he was in during the war, the car factory he worked in afterwards and…' (Danny threw it in for a bit of colour) 'from his fellow inmates at Wormwood Scrubs.' He paused for a moment and looked up at Professor Moon. She seemed to be lapping it all up. At least, there were no obvious signs of disbelief on her face.

'Thing is, we'd *really* like to find out a bit more about his knife.' Danny handed over the photo. 'It was given to him by a wounded Moroccan Goumier whose life he saved by carrying him away from a German advance. Grandpa says Jerry didn't take the Goumiers prisoner. Just gunned 'em down like dogs.' Danny paused and shot a quick glance into Professor Moon's eyes. He was starting to think he might be making old Grandpa a little too colourful as her eyebrows had raised themselves a few millimetres.

'Anyway,' he carried on, a little nervously, 'it looks like an antique and we thought it might be valuable or at least interesting, or something.' Realising he was starting to babble, he shut up and looked expectantly at the Professor as she studied the photo.

'Hmm, I think…' she said, almost to herself, 'yes, I'm sure I've seen one like this before… wait a minute.' Pulling down a thick textbook from a high shelf, she flipped through it for a moment. 'Yes, here we are.' She turned the book around so that it was facing Danny and pointed at an image at the centre of the page. 'This is an Amazigh koumyia dating from the nineteenth century, very similar to your great-grandfather's dagger. Note the peculiarly intricate silver work on the pommel and the polished cedar-wood grip. Even the shape of the blade is extraordinarily similar. This example,' she turned the book back towards herself to read the description, 'belonged to an infamous Amazigh bandit called Rissouli.'

'Cool! Really? Do you think grandpa's dagger might have belonged to a bandit?' asked Danny, knowing of course, that it had belonged to a murderer only very recently.

Professor Moon laughed, 'Well, maybe. There's no real way of telling. I can tell you that Rissouli's dagger is believed to have been made by artisans in Chefchaoen, in the Rif Mountains of Morocco. Rissouli ran his criminal empire from Chefchaoen, so that would make sense. The similarities in your great-grandfather's dagger would suggest it was made by the same artisans, probably around the same period.'

'So the Goumier that Grandpa rescued might have been connected to Rissouli's gang?'

'Possibly only in a very loose sense. Rissouli was killed in 1867 by French soldiers, and his gang is thought to have disbanded not long afterwards. I suppose there's a chance that the Goumier may have been the descendant of a gang member.' Professor Moon smiled and stood up. 'I should really be getting on with some work now, I'm afraid that's about as much as I can tell you.'

'No, that's great, thank you,' said Danny. 'That's much more interesting than I'd ever hoped for.'

Danny had not only confirmed the dagger was Moroccan, but he'd narrowed it down to the town where it had probably been made, and established that it might even have had criminal connections. Perhaps the descendants of Rissouli's gang were still operating in modern day Morocco? It was an interesting thought and one he could not wait to tell Angus.

★ ★ ★

While Danny had been charming Professor Moon, Angus had been peering through the reinforced glass window of a laboratory door in North London. Now, at last, he took a deep breath and pushed the door open. 'Hello, Cate.'

Cate turned, flicking her hair behind her left ear as she did so. 'How come you only call me when you want to talk shop?' she said, a little grumpily.

Angus didn't really have an answer for that and reddened a little. Cate was far prettier than a forensic scientist ought to be. Five foot three in her canvas pumps, her loosely curled dark hair fell softly to her shoulders, framing her clear, green eyes and a smile that could break a man's heart at fifty paces.

'Ah, never mind. I have discovered an interesting little coincidence that I'm sure you'll appreciate.' She turned and picked up a report from her worktop.

'Really? I was hoping you'd say something like that,' said Angus.

'Yes, I've compared the samples of drugs seized from the dealer who shot Desray with those taken from the gang boss who was arrested for speeding. Their merchandise came from a variety of sources. We can tell that by its chemical composition. For example, Desray's killer got his cocaine from Columbia, whereas the other chap got his from Ecuador. However, both got their cannabis resin from the same source.'

'Are you sure?' asked Angus, impressed.

'Pretty much. I've analysed samples of the resin and discovered they both contain identical proportions of trace cannabinoids in comparison to tetrahydrocannabinol and relatively low concentrations of Cannabidiol, which… Angus! Try to concentrate.'

'I *am* concentrating!'

'Your eyes were glazing over by the time I got to 'trace cannabinoids'.'

'Do you blame me?' Angus grinned. All this was way over his head but he had always found Cate's enthusiasm for anything scientific to be incredibly appealing.

'No, I suppose not,' she replied. 'I guess the point I'm trying to make is that cannabis resin varies in its make-up depending on where it's grown and how it's processed. Cannabis resin from two different sources would never be as similar as these two samples. Therefore both dealers got their cannabis from the same source.'

'I don't suppose you'd be able to tell me where that source is?'

'Yes, in fact I can!' she smiled and hugged the report to her chest with pleasure. 'North Africa. Probably West. Morocco or Algeria most likely.'

Angus smiled slowly; this could be the link he was looking for. All three cases were connected by Brunton handguns, and now that two of them were connected by one North African drugs supplier, perhaps some connection between the Thames floater and the drugs would be found. He threw one last look into Cate's green eyes and then glanced down at his watch.

'Look, I've got to go and meet Danny, thanks for everything. You've been great, as always!'

'I expect dinner out of this. At the very least!' she called after him as he strode out of her lab.

'It's a deal! Somewhere nice too…' and he was off.

CHAPTER TWO

After Danny and Angus had compared notes, their course of action became clear. All three cases were obviously connected to Brunton by the handguns, but also to North-West Africa by the cannabis and the dagger. If Professor Moon was right about the dagger, they could narrow this down to Chefchaouen in Morocco's Rif Mountains. The next step was to go to Chefchaouen and see what they could find out on the spot. Newby had given them the name of a man he knew from 'the old days', who would be their contact in Chefchaouen. Quite when the 'old days' had been and what had happened during them, Newby would not tell them. He had merely rumbled: 'Just be careful. He's an old friend of mine, so you should be all right, but beneath all that smooth bonhomie he's still an old rogue, a thief and smuggler!'

★ ★ ★

Two days later they were back in Dunkeld, loading up Angus's pick-up for the journey south. Danny eyed the truck with disfavour. It was an old Toyota Hi-Lux that had been red, before the years of sun, wind and rain had faded it to a shade of pink. To make matters worse, Angus had not bothered to remove the previous owner's business name, meaning that Danny had to ride around in a vehicle whose sides were emblazoned with:

Auchtermuchty Drainage Engineers. Your Sewage Is Our Bread and Butter.

Angus was clearly having the time of his life, however, and had spent most of the morning bolting big aluminium boxes into the back of the pick-up and clipping shovels and things called 'sand-ladders' to the side. Larger desert wheels were fitted and two spares strapped into the back, next to the jerry cans containing emergency supplies of diesel and water.

Around lunchtime Angus pealed off his filthy old overalls and sat down on his pile of sand in the yard. Danny handed him a mug of what Angus called 'industry standard tea' (milk, two sugars) and asked: 'Finished?'

'I think so. Can't think of anything I might have forgotten. My maps of the area are a bit out of date, but there's no time to get more.'

'Are you seriously saying we are going to take that…er…' Danny searched for words that would adequately convey his reservations about the vehicle. 'That wheezing old rust-bucket into the depths of the Sahara?'

'We might not need to. I'm just taking the extra gear in case. Anyway, it's not a wheezing old rust-bucket. It may be a little 'visually challenged', shall we say, but these things are almost entirely indestructible. You can keep your Chelsea tractors; stone age simplicity and no nonsense toughness are what you need in the desert.'

'Maybe, although a Chelsea tractor would have air-conditioning.'

Angus laughed, 'I guess so! You packed?'

Danny nodded.

'Good, then let's get some lunch and go. It's a four day drive to Morocco.'

★ ★ ★

Driving south through the UK was the usual battle with road works, traffic-jams and limp egg sandwiches from overcrowded service stations. Eventually, when they reached Dover, Angus visibly relaxed, as though the white cliffs were a signal to him that another adventure was about to begin.

Danny wondered, as they drove down the hill to the ferry terminal, how many other grand adventures had begun here. From military campaigns to secret missions, from great explorations to little personal adventures: how many people had stood under those cliffs with the same tingle of excitement in their gut, wondering what their futures held... perhaps some even wondering if they would ever see those cliffs again?

Danny shuddered at this thought. Did he really know what he was getting himself into? Suddenly he realised that he was about to take on drug smugglers, gun-runners and murderers armed with little more than a Swiss army knife and an exhaustive knowledge of *The Simpsons*. A surge of panic welled up in his chest and he looked across at Angus, to see how he was taking it.

His uncle was happily stuffing another egg sandwich into his mouth and humming along to the radio.

'*Fanbwidge?*' Angus said, barely squeezing the word out past the egg and bread.

'I'm sorry?' replied Danny. 'You practicing your French already?'

'Fanbwidge?' Angus repeated, losing a little bit of egg onto his shirt this time and holding out the plastic box containing lunch.

'Oh, you mean 'sandwich'? Thanks!' Danny laughed and instantly felt better. He knew it may be optimistic, but he felt certain that as long as he stuck by Angus everything would be all right.

★ ★ ★

The short ferry journey offered a break from being stuck in the cramped Toyota. Leaning over the rail in the fresh light wind, they watched the waves being churned up by the propeller as England retreated over the horizon.

In no time they were back in the cab and driving out the dark bowels of the ferry in a rumbling mass of trucks, cars and motorbikes, out into the French sunshine.

The drive through France almost felt like a holiday: the sun shone, and they stopped in little roadside 'aires' to eat pain au chocolat and baguettes with soft cheese. Nearby, families spread vast picnics on red gingham tablecloths and cackled and gesticulated in the dappled sunlight below the trees.

Not far south of Nimes they crested a low rise and got their first glimpse of the Pyrenees. The rugged brown peaks, still streaked with the winter's snow, dominated the horizon in front of them. Near Montpellier they caught sight of the Mediterranean, a much more vivid blue, Danny thought, than the English

Channel. A blustery wind whipped the waves into foam in the bays and rolled the little fishing boats on their moorings.

Climbing up into the Pyrenees, the roads became narrower and more winding. They passed through tiny villages which seemed draped in a cloak of antiquity. Narrow streets, often cobbled with stones polished smooth by centuries of use, twisted between the closely-huddled, squat little houses. There were faded adverts for Martell Cognac peeling from the walls of barns, and weather-beaten shutters rattled at the windows. Every village had a boulangerie, a mangy cat and a rusty Citroen 2CV in its square. Danny thought it strange that the scenery seemed to be getting more French with every mile they got closer to leaving France.

When they reached the top of the pass Danny and Angus looked south into Spain. It wasn't long before there was a noticeable change in the landscape; it was just as ruggedly beautiful here, but it was much drier and browner. Arid mountains rose up amongst the plains of vines and fruit trees. The remains of Moorish forts scattered the landscape like broken teeth. The air was hotter and drier and the sun appeared higher in the sky.

That night Danny and Angus camped on the shores of the Mediterranean. After dinner (sausages, beans and fried eggs again), Danny sat on the beach and stared up at the stars. The scent of the sea mingled with that of the orange grove behind him. Out at sea, in the darkness, the navigation lights of dozens of boats winked like a string of Christmas lights, green, red and orange. Above him, Orion, one of the two constellations he could recognize, pointed his sword through the darkness towards Africa.

Danny stared into the night, worried about what lay ahead. What would they find down there in Africa? His uncle always seemed so calm about the future, content to deal with problems as they arose. But Danny could not help turning things over in his head, and worrying about the possibilities. It was only the fear of the unknown, he decided. He had never been on an investigation before, so had no idea what to expect. Angus, he realised, was completely at ease because he had spent years doing just this kind of thing. So if *he* knew what to expect and wasn't scared, then there was nothing to be scared about. Cheered by this thought Danny got up, dusted the sand off his jeans and headed back to the tent.

★ ★ ★

The next morning they got up early to catch the first ferry over to Morocco. They carried on down the coast, through the increasingly crowded towns and tourist resorts of the Costa del Sol. It was another baking hot day so they drove with the windows open, leaning their arms out to catch the breeze. The wait at the ferry terminal was mercifully short and they were soon sailing out of Algericas and on their way to Morocco.

Danny stared out of the windows at the front of the ferry, waiting eagerly for his first glimpse of Africa. Around him was a jumble of European tourists, truck drivers, homeward-bound

Moroccans and their luggage. It seemed incredible to him that he was actually here. Within a couple of hours he would be standing on African soil, having come overland all the way from Scotland. He was starting to understand why Angus always tried to travel on the surface of the earth, rather than in the air. It gave you a sense of scale and place; it showed just how vast the world was, and exactly where you were in it. Danny remembered Angus saying once, 'The only people who say 'It's a small world' are those who haven't driven across a continent.'

★ ★ ★

Angus cleared the hurly-burly of customs with the expertise of a man well-used to such bureaucratic shenanigans. A few well placed Euros, smiles and small talk to the appropriate officials and they were soon out of the gates and into Morocco. It could have been his imagination, but when they disembarked Danny felt sure it was hotter already. Although the journey across the Straits of Gibraltar had only taken half an hour, and they were still just twenty miles from Europe, he thought there was something dustier and more punishing about the heat.

★ ★ ★

They took the coastal road, signposted to Tetouan, in the early afternoon. Danny had never been out of Europe before and now here he was, driving through Africa. He leant out of the open window, returning the occasional wave from the Moroccans. Most of the cars here were Mercedes, old beige taxis with tasselled ornaments swinging from their rear-view mirrors and large numbers of people crammed into their back seats. Here and there were scooters and the odd donkey. The locals themselves wore disappointingly Western clothing. Danny saw one young man in an Arsenal shirt and two more who appeared to be Manchester United fans.

After a while, their road turned away from the coast and rose into surprisingly green hills. They battled through the noisy traffic of Tetouan, where the road rules seemed to be 'just keep pushing forward until everyone gets out of your way' and men on motorcycles buzzed around them, trying to get them to visit their carpet shop, café or hotel. Eventually they found their way out of Tetouan's sprawling mass and headed south for Chefchaouen.

The road became steeper, passing signposts for places with long and mysterious names, like Dar-Ben-Karriche-El-Bahri and Souk-el-Arba-des-Beni-Hassan.

The sun was just kissing the horizon when they arrived in the outskirts of Chefchaouen. Surrounded by wooded hills and overlooked by the white minaret of a hilltop mosque, the pale blue houses looked far too peaceful and respectable to be hiding murderous criminals.

Danny and Angus pulled up, as had been agreed, in the square in front of the main entrance to the medina and stepped out to stretch and yawn away the stiffness in their limbs. As they did so, a man in a suit detached himself from the wall he was leaning against and strolled over.

'You,' he said with a grin, jabbing his forefinger at him, 'must be Angus! Welcome my friend!'

'As-Sal mu `Alayka, and you must be Mohammed,' replied Angus, shaking hands with the barrel-chested Moroccan. Mohammed was not terribly tall, but what he lacked in height he more than made up for in width. Aged somewhere in his fifties, his bulk was not all muscle but it had been once, and the confident way he carried himself hinted that he might still prove a formidably tough customer.

Mohammed was grinning at Danny now, a gold tooth flashing in burning reflection of the setting sun. Placing a huge and heavy hand on Danny's head, he ruffled his hair and laughed. 'You must be the one I have been told to keep a close eye on! Come, let us go to my little home in the suburbs!'

Mohammed's 'little home in the suburbs' turned out to be a sprawling villa with a large walled garden, on the Southern outskirts of the town. They sat on the veranda in the warm night air and discussed the situation over a lamb tajine.

After a little explanation Angus got down to the nitty-gritty. 'So, as you can see, it's a pretty tenuous link, but it's all we've got so far. We know the cannabis was grown around here and…jings, this tajine is lovely…' Angus paused to take another mouthful, 'where was I? Oh yes, the dagger. Made right here in Chefchaouen, or so our research indicates. It's very similar to one owned by the nineteenth century bandit, Rissouli.' A final forkful disappeared into Angus's mouth and he sat back, chewing and regarding Mohammed questioningly.

'Rissouli!' Mohammed chuckled softly, staring with unfocused eyes into the past. 'Rissouli, eh? So that is who is behind this smuggling of yours...'

'Rissouli has been dead for one hundred and forty years,' Angus reminded him gently.

'True. True indeed. But his gang? No! His gang remain, my friend! They are a thorn in my side this very day.'

'Isn't it true that Rissouli's gang were destroyed by the French?' asked Angus, intrigued.

'Ah, no. Rissouli himself was killed, and many of his gang died with him. The few survivors were scattered to the four winds. Some went south, disappearing into the Sahara. Others went east to Algeria and a few even went north into Europe. The French authorities assumed the gang had been smashed forever. But we Amazigh are tough old foxes, my friends. Slowly the gang reformed, more secretive and more dangerous than before. Calling themselves the 'Sons of Rissouli' they have smuggled and stolen and murdered across the whole of West Africa for over a century. If there is devilry in this country it is always likely that the Sons of Rissouli are part of it!'

Mohammed's expression became more serious as he continued, 'They are clever, these men, they do not advertise their existence to the authorities and so remain unmolested by the police. But exist they do. And I know because I have more than once had to, how do you say... 'negotiate' with them.' He leaned forward, hunching his shoulders and staring darkly at Angus. 'Negotiate...yes, negotiate in blood!'

There was an uncomfortable silence for a moment as he held

Angus's gaze, then suddenly he relaxed. 'Pah!' he said, waving his hand dismissively and breaking into a smile again. 'These dogs are scum. Cruel and treacherous, they would smuggle anything you like to the highest bidder, steal food from the starving or medicines from the sick, and yes, even kill for the fun of it. They are a stain on my community and I will do all I can to help you crush them!'

Danny watched Mohammed with fascination. Newby had told them a little about the man before they left, and he knew Mohammed to be a smuggler and one-time camel thief himself. But here was clearly a man of honour and character, a man who probably found cruelty and murder as abhorrent as Danny and Angus did. Mohammed could be the vital link they needed to find out exactly how those guns were making it back into Britain.

'Do you know where these 'Sons of Rissouli' are based?' asked Angus.

'But of course. They have a house in the highest part of the old medina, right here in Chefchaouen.'

'Excellent. Do you think you could show us where it is? Later tonight, when the moon has gone in.'

Mohammed's eyes twinkled in the lamplight and he smiled conspiratorially. 'Ah, you are thinking to take a closer look, no? Certainly I can show you. It will be fun!'

★ ★ ★

It was well after midnight when the moon dipped behind the

black hills around the town. There had been some discussion over whether Danny should be coming with them. His pleas to be included had been steadfastly refused by Angus until Mohammed had promised that one of his men would come and keep a close eye on the boy.

'My best man, Aghilas, will protect the boy with his life,' he pledged. 'Angus, the boy must become a man some day. At his age I was stealing camels from under the very noses of the toughest Amazigh chiefs in Morocco!' he said, laughing aloud at the memory.

So, with some reluctance, Angus had agreed that Danny could come. In dark clothing they stole into the medina from the south-west, far from the main entrance; not sneaking, just walking quietly as though they had every reason to be there. There were a few electric lights, fed by tangles of ancient wire, but much of the medina was in darkness, leaving them to feel their way slowly down the narrow, stone-flagged streets. Climbing north they were glad of Mohammed's guidance. The tiny streets and alleys diverged, criss-crossed and wandered through the tightly packed houses in such a confusing way that only someone with an intimate knowledge of them would be able to find their way in the dark.

Eventually, as they approached a place where the streets widened, Mohammed held up his hand in signal for them to halt. He then indicated that they should fall back against a nearby wall, close in amongst the shadows.

'Round this corner,' whispered Mohammed, 'you'll see a large square building. These are the headquarters of the Sons of Rissouli.'

Angus edged to the corner and peered around, watching motionlessly for a minute. The building was indeed large and square. It had small windows, high up and a heavy-looking door with ornate iron hinges and a brass knocker in the shape of a hand. Interestingly, it was the only building that Angus had seen in the medina that stood alone from its neighbours. Narrow lanes disappeared into darkness on either side. Neither was lit, making Angus wonder if the gang kept them that way for a reason.

There were no lights on in the building either and no vehicles were parked in front.

Angus motioned Mohammed forward. 'Looks pretty quiet,' he whispered. 'Do you think there might be no-one home?'

Mohammed peered round the corner before replying. 'Their cars are not there; perhaps they are away on business. I would imagine they have left one or two men on guard, however.'

Smiling at Mohammed's use of the expression 'away on business', Angus said, 'Look, we might never get another chance this good. I'm going to see if I can get inside. Do you know a better way in? This looks a little exposed.'

'Yes, I can take you to the back, follow me,' said Mohammed, heading for a small alley they had passed on their way up to the house.

★ ★ ★

Five minutes later, after a confusing journey along lanes

that got progressively narrower and darker, they arrived at the back of the house. It was deathly quiet there; so quiet that Danny could hear the others breathing as they stared at the window. Danny kept shooting glances up and down the alley. It seemed like an awful place to attempt a break-in. If the Sons of Rissouli thugs came at them from both sides, they would be trapped. They could be beaten to death in this filthy, cramped, black slit of an alley, Danny thought. Would anyone ever know what happened to them, or would the Sons of Rissouli simply take their corpses out into the desert for the vultures to pick clean?

Meanwhile, in the curious silent telepathy that develops in situations like this, Angus placed a hand on Aghilas' shoulder, touched his own chest, then pointed at the window. Aghilas nodded and crouched by the wall, where Angus, now with an open penknife held between his teeth, climbed onto his back until he was standing on his shoulders. Rising slowly, Aghilas raised Angus till he could reach the window-ledge.

Danny watched as, with a low grunt of effort, Angus pulled himself up and rapidly pulled open the window and disappeared from view.

There was a soft chuckle from Mohammed. 'Heh, heh. Your uncle… This is not his first break-in, I think!' Danny could make out just enough in the darkness to see Mohammed wink at him.

It was an unpleasantly hot and sticky night; crouching in the shadows of that narrow lane, waiting for Angus to reappear, felt like doing time at the bottom of a well. Looking up, he could see a thin line of stars in the narrow gap between the neighbouring roofs, but this only served to increase the sense of claustrophobia.

As the minutes ticked by, a feeling that something was going to go wrong kept nagging at him. Angus seemed to be taking forever, what could be taking so long? He was sure it was getting hotter; the filth and the dust were tickling his throat and eventually he had to stifle a cough.

'Shh!' hissed Mohammed.

'Sorry...' Danny murmured back.

'No, it's OK,' Mohammed laid a hand on Danny's shoulder. 'I thought I heard footsteps coming this way. Quick, Aghilas, this is no place for the boy, take him to the Plaza Uta el-Hammam, we will meet by the Grand Mosque.'

'Should we not wait for Angus?' asked Danny. He wanted nothing more than to get the hell out of there, but he didn't want to leave without Angus.

'It is fine,' replied Mohammed. 'I will…' He paused; from the blackest shadows of the alley to their right had come a sound, like the rustle of hurried footsteps. They all froze, staring into the darkness, trying in vain to see what had made the noise. Danny could feel his heart pounding against his chest and a cold bead of sweat trickling slowly down his back. Every second groaned past like a century. Another sound came from the darkness; a sound uncomfortably like a knife being drawn from a sheath. A dark figure stepped from the shadows, tall and thin and swathed in a hooded djellaba, in his hand a long curved dagger. Danny stared, it looked exactly like the dagger which had been stuck in the man found floating in the Thames.

Then, from behind them, came a sound even more chilling than that of a knife being drawn: a low and menacing laugh. Whirling around, they saw another silhouette shrouded in a djellaba the same colour as the night. He too was brandishing a long, curved dagger. The sinister shadow spoke, in a slow, guttural whisper: 'The Sons of Rissouli do not tolerate such violation. For this you must die!'

At this moment everything exploded into chaotic action. Mohammed roared: 'ANGUS! TIME TO GO!' and with a bellow charged the man, hitting him like an express train. They fell to the gutter in a struggling, swearing mass, the attacker's dagger clattering across the cobbles as Mohammed knocked it from his grasp.

Aghilas grabbed Danny and pushed him against the wall, then turned to stand between him and the other figure. There was a sharp metallic click and suddenly a long slim blade appeared in Aghilas' hand, its polished edge gleaming silver in the starlight. He watched as the dark silhouettes of the two men met, became indistinguishable for a moment, and then separated as the thug slid to the ground with a gurgling sigh.

As Danny stared horrified at the crumpled figure lying motionless where he had fallen, he felt a strong hand grab him by the arm and start dragging him from the spot.

'Come, quickly!' hissed Aghilas, 'We must go!'

'But...' said Danny, looking back at where Mohammed was still struggling with the other attacker.

'I have my orders to keep you safe, now come!'

And so Danny found himself pounding back through the medina, running as hard as he could, heart racing and lungs bursting with the effort. Alleys they had crept through silently less than an hour before they now charged down, helter-skelter with no heed to silence or concealment. Soon, he had no idea where they were and just kept running after Aghilas through the tangle of tiny streets. Once the streets widened and there were more electric lights they slowed to a walk. After another fifty yards they came out on a large, open square bordered by shuttered cafes on one side and a mosque on the other.

There was nobody about, as it was the middle of the night, but Danny actually felt safer. There was an air of normality here; it didn't have the sinister, anonymous feel of the darkened alleys. Without a word to each other, Danny and Aghilas crept over to one of the trees growing close to the mosque and sat down under it to wait for the others, becoming invisible in its shadow.

★ ★ ★

When Angus pulled himself up to the window ledge he was pleased to see a rickety window locked with an old hook and eye latch. In his experience, gangsters rarely bothered with up-to-date security equipment. After all, what burglar would rob a house full of people who would not just kill him, but kill him in an imaginative manner?

Slipping the blade of his penknife in the crack between the window frames he flicked the hook out of the eye and pulled the window open. In a move that rock climbers call a 'mantel-shelf', he pulled himself into a position where he could get first one foot, then the other onto the window-ledge, then jumped lightly down into the pitch black room.

He waited motionless, listening… no sound at all could be heard in the hot and heavy night air. Crouching close to the floor, completely blind in the darkness, he put out his hands and felt the rough weave of a Moroccan carpet. He waited another few seconds before standing up and reaching into his pocket. Attached to his car keys was a tiny torch. Flicking it on, he found himself in a small storage room. It contained grubby cardboard boxes, old carpets, broken furniture and fat cockroaches which scuttled away as the torchlight swept over them. He took a quick look through some of the boxes but they were filled with nothing but junk. No, he decided, there was nothing in here of interest. He would have to explore the house a little more.

He switched off his torch, opened the door and peered out. Like many houses in Morocco, this one had been built around a central courtyard that was open to the sky. In the starlight, Angus could see that it was four storeys high, with walkways at each level connected by ornate wooden staircases. Lining the walkways were heavy-looking wooden doors, behind which would be bedrooms, toilets, or living rooms. But Angus was looking for a study or office where he would find evidence of gun-running. Of course, a store room full of Brunton weaponry would be nice too, but he doubted the gang would keep anything like that here.

Angus decided to ignore the rooms on the ground floor;

that would be where the kitchen, washroom and servants' quarters would be. The first and second floors would probably be where the more lowly hoodlums lived. The boss's rooms were most likely to be at the top, so Angus decided to start there.

Pausing every few moments to listen, he slowly climbed up the ancient stairs, which creaked horribly with every step. He expected a door to burst open, a light to shine on him and a hail of bullets to bring a premature end to his career as a brilliant young journalist.

However, he reached the top floor without incident and stood for a moment in the cool breeze. There were fewer doors on this floor, suggesting bigger rooms behind them, which fitted with his guess that they belonged to the house's most important resident.

He crept over to the first door and turned the handle gently. There was a soft 'clunk' before he pushed open the door just wide enough that he could slip inside, and then closed it behind him. In the soft starlight filtering in through the window he could just about make out a bed, which thankfully appeared to be empty. Switching on his torch for a better look, he swept its beam quickly across the room to confirm he was alone.

The room was luxuriously and traditionally furnished. Thick woollen carpets covered the floor, with several intricately carved chests of drawers along the walls. There was a small table and a couple of chairs near the bed. It was huge cast iron sort and the only thing in the room that looked European. It had been turned down with crisp linen sheets (presumably by a servant. Angus doubted that there was a gang boss anywhere in the world who made his own bed).

Rifling quickly through the chests of drawers he found nothing but some clothes and other personal possessions. Working on a sudden hunch he swept his hand under the pillows on the bed. Sure enough his hand brushed against something cold and hard. He knew what it was before he pulled it out to look at it. A gun. Examining it in the light of his torch he read the etching on its slide: 'Brunton 9mm'.

'So...The Sons of Rissouli *are* connected to the gun smuggling.' he muttered to himself, sliding it back under the pillow. For a gun as rare as a Brunton to have been here by coincidence was too much to believe. He looked at the luminous dial of his watch. Time was passing quickly and he still had to find out how they were getting hold of the guns and smuggling them back into Europe.

Leaving the bedroom he sneaked to the next door on the landing. It looked like it was a living room, with low seats and tables. The next was a tiled bathroom, which left just one more room to investigate.

Angus eased open the final door and glanced inside. *This is more promising*, he thought. It was an office with a window that faced out over the back of the building, directly over where the others would be waiting. He pushed it open and looked down, but could see no-one. There wasn't much furniture here, just a substantial wooden desk, a leather chair and a low cabinet that contained smoking paraphernalia and a few bottles of whisky and gin. The desk drawers had nothing more incriminating in them than some bank statements. The figures showed a business called Compagnie Dakar Expedition was raking in large amounts of money and distributing it to lots of other accounts, but Angus could learn nothing about how the company generated its income. However, he took a quick note of the name in the hope that Mohammed would recognise it.

It was a pretty disappointing result; clearly the Sons of Rissouli were careful about covering their tracks.

As he was about to leave, he spotted a pad on the desk. More in hope than in expectation, he removed the top sheet and tucked it carefully into his shirt pocket. Just then he heard two things almost simultaneously: the creak of a footfall on the staircase swiftly followed by Mohammed's shout: 'ANGUS! TIME TO GO!'

This was clearly no time to muck around. Angus ran to the door, throwing it open with a crash. Almost before he realised it, he had thrown a hard punch into the face of a grinning thug who had appeared outside. He had taken the hulking figure by surprise, catching him square on the bridge of the nose. With a 'crack!' he fell backwards, but he was a big man and one punch wasn't going to put him down for long. As soon as he hit the floor, he was raising himself from it. Angus lashed out with his right foot, catching him under the chin with the toe of his desert boot. The thug's head snapped back, his eyes rolled in his head and he slumped to the floor unconscious.

Angus ran to the stairs and charged down three steps at a time. Thinking fast, he decided the best route out was the one he had come in, that way he could lend a hand if Mohammed, Aghilas and Danny were in trouble.

Reaching the store room, he crashed through the door and ran to the window. Looking down he could see a lifeless form in a dark djellaba slumped in the gutter. Ten yards away, he could just make out two men. One appeared to have his arm wrapped around the other's throat in a choke hold. As Angus jumped down he realised, with relief, that this was Mohammed. As he reached the struggling pair, the thug went limp and Mohammed released his hold, letting him fall to the ground.

'Mohammed, what happened here?'

Mohammed turned and, panting heavily, offered a weak smile. 'We were ambushed, Aghilas dealt with the other one,' he indicated the body in the gutter, 'and left with Danny for the Plaza Uta el-Hammam.'

Angus indicated the man at Mohammed's feet. 'Is he dead?'

'No, but he will feel pretty bad in the morning,' replied Mohammed as he crossed to where the other man lay. Bending over, he pressed his fingers to the man's neck. 'His friend was not so lucky. Aghilas is a bad man to cross.'

Angus nodded, 'Come on, let's get to the Plaza. I want to make sure Danny is safe.'

They hurried back through the twisting maze, Mohammed flagging a little now, after such a hard night for a man of his age. Angus was silent, too wrapped in his own thoughts to speak. Breaking into the house had seemed a good idea at the time. How many of the stupid, dangerous situations that he had got himself into over the years had 'seemed like a good idea at the time'? He knew he really ought to think things out first. Now a man was dead, and for what? For a few bank details which would probably lead to nothing. Angus cursed himself again and wondered if Danny was all right. He would never forgive himself if the boy had been hurt too.

★ ★ ★

Sitting under the tree in the Plaza, Danny shivered against the cold as a light wind blew through his sweat-soaked clothes. His mind was still a tumbling mess of thoughts and questions as he struggled to make sense of what had just happened. Angus breaking into the house was a little scary, but it was exciting. He knew what his uncle would say about it: 'It had certainly seemed like a good idea at the time.'

However, when the henchmen had arrived everything had changed. Suddenly Danny realised just how nasty and dangerous this could get. Had he just seen a man being killed? That gurgling sigh was the most horrible sound he had ever heard. He shuddered and tried not to think about it. He could not believe Angus, that affable, loveable rogue, did something as terrifying as this for a living. To do this once was madness, but to do it repeatedly, time after time, year after year...? Danny was fast coming to the conclusion that his uncle should be locked up for his own safety.

It wasn't more than a few minutes before Angus and Mohammed arrived, breathing heavily. Angus hurried over to Danny, concern written across his face.

'Are you OK? Sorry about that, it all went a bit haywire.'

Danny eyed Angus critically. 'Physically, I'm fine,' he replied sourly. 'But I expect I'll be mentally scarred for bleeding life.'

Angus laughed. It was a laugh of relief rather than amusement. 'Good!' he said. 'But don't worry about those sorts of scars, lad, they are what make us interesting!'

CHAPTER THREE

Back at the villa, they sat in Mohammed's study wondering what to make of the business name Angus had found. Mohammed had not heard of Compagnie Dakar Expedition, but thought it sounded like a haulage company; a useful business to be in if you were smuggling arms and drugs.

'Well, there's not much more we can do tonight...' Angus said and then stopped, reaching into his top pocket. 'Wait a minute. I tore this off a notepad in the house.' He laid the piece of paper out on the desk.

'But, my friend, it is blank.' Mohammed looked puzzled. He could not see how this could be of any help.

Angus grinned, 'It's an old trick, but a good one. Have you got a pencil? The softer the better.'

Mohammed reached into a drawer and produced one. Taking the pencil, Angus held it almost flat to the paper and rubbed it gently across the sheet, as if shading a drawing. As he did, a faint row of numbers appeared.

'Like I say, it's an old trick, but it's not the first time it's worked for me!' laughed Angus. 'You see, when you write on a pad you make an impression on the sheets below. Shading the paper with a pencil makes it stand out,' he explained.

As Angus, Mohammed and Aghilas leant over the desk to study the scrap of paper in the light of a desk lamp, Danny sat back in a leather armchair. He worried he had been getting in the way since they arrived in Morocco. Sure, back in England he had managed to blag some good information from Professor Moon, but since then it seemed his only contribution had been to correct Angus's lamentable navigation on the journey through Europe. With this and other uncomfortable thoughts flitting through his head like shadows in the night, his eyelids grew heavy and he was soon lost in a fitful sleep.

★ ★ ★

'Danny…Danny…Oi! Wake up you lazy bum!'

He opened his eyes to see bright sunshine streaming through the window of the study. Angus was standing over him with a cup of hot, sweet mint tea.

'Get this down you and join us on the veranda for breakfast.'

Danny rubbed his eyes and stretched, stiff from sleeping curled up in the chair. 'What time is it?'

'Ten o'clock. C'mon, or it will all be gone.'

Out on the veranda Mohammed and Aghilas were already tucking into a fine spread of bread, butter and jam.

Danny sat down. 'What are we going to do today then? I'd like to avoid almost being murdered by a gang of hoodlums if that's all right with you?'

Angus grinned, 'Well, I can't guarantee anything but I'll do my best! Actually, I'm not sure where to go from here. We're still no closer to knowing what this number means.'

He laid the scrap of paper on the table in front of Danny.

Danny looked carefully at the long number faintly

visible amongst the grey mass of pencil shading. He rested a contemplative finger against the side of his nose and sighed. Ten numbers in a row. What could it mean? It didn't look like a phone number. He supposed it could be a bank account... As he looked, however, he noticed something else. The gap between the fifth number and the sixth number was slightly larger than those between all the other numbers. He looked again, more closely. This wasn't one ten digit number! Suddenly it all made sense and he knew exactly what he was looking at.

Grinning like the Cheshire cat he calmly put the paper down and started spreading butter on his bread. The three men stared at him expectantly, wondering what he was smiling about. But he was going to enjoy keeping them in suspense as long as he could.

Eventually Angus cracked. 'Well?' he asked.

'Well, what?' said Danny innocently, reaching for the jam.

'Well, what are you looking so pleased about?'

'Oh, I'm grinning because…' Danny paused as he struggled to unscrew the lid of the jar. 'Ah, there it goes. Mmm, strawberry, my favourite. Have you got a favourite jam, Angus?'

'Look, spit it out will you. Why the hell are you grinning so much?'

Danny laughed. 'I'm grinning 'cos I know what the number is!'

'Really? Well, if you'd like to share your knowledge we'd all be very grateful.'

'OK then. For a starter it's not one long number. They are two separate numbers. And what's more, they're directions. A longitude and latitude, a position on a map. Like you would put into a GPS.'

Angus snatched up the paper and looked at it again. 'Holy cow, Danny, I think you might be right! Why didn't I think of that?'

'Well I wouldn't like to say,' said Danny, inspecting his fingernails. It was good to feel useful again. Perhaps he had even broken the case? He was feeling the same rush of excitement as when he had walked out of Professor Moon's office what seemed like months ago. Was it really only last week? Danny was beginning to understand why Angus had chosen to live like this. Sure there were scary, dangerous moments but you didn't half feel like you were living life!

Angus was already spreading a map out on the table. Running his fingers across its expanse his hand moved quickly south and east, almost off the bottom right-hand corner of the map. 'If they are co-ordinates, then they indicate a position right about… here. Unfortunately 'here' is about thirty kilometres over the Algerian border.'

Angus pointed to an area on the map that was almost devoid of markings, apart from a tiny blue dot, the symbol for a well.

Mohammed spoke up. 'I know this place. It is the only well in the area, a natural stopping point if you were heading south for Mauritania. Do not worry that it is in Algeria, the desert is without people here. You could drive there without seeing a soul. Perhaps that is why the Sons of Rissouli are using it?' He smiled knowingly.

'Maybe this is where the rest of the gang were last night?' asked Danny. 'They could have been given this location by someone as a place to meet?'

'That's definitely a possibility,' replied Angus. Folding up the map, he made a decision. 'Right, get your stuff, Danny. We're leaving for Algeria!'

★ ★ ★

Half an hour later, after saying their goodbyes and giving their thanks to Mohammed and Aghilas, Danny and Angus were on the road south again. Passing the historic town of Fes, they climbed into the foothills of the Atlas and stayed overnight in Azrou, surrounded by green forested hills. The following day, after an early breakfast of flatbread and jam from one of the tiny, cupboard-sized shops that were everywhere in Morocco, they carried on. South through the mountains, south again to the desert. And not just any desert, thought Danny, this was the king of all deserts: The Sahara! Danny's mind swam with images of the famous desert he had seen in books and on TV. Rolling, endless dunes of golden sand, tiny oases of palms and clear water, camels ridden by Tuareg raiders with long flintlock rifles… what would the reality be? Well, he would soon find out; according to Angus they would be there that evening.

Before long, they dropped down into the wide Ziz valley, which snaked its way in an elongated oasis between the dry mountains. The Ziz, a ribbon of brown water, flowed between green plantations of date palms where mud-brick houses squatted among the trees and close to the water, close to the source of life.

They stopped in a village just past Er-Rachida to buy bread and cheese for lunch. This was the Morocco of Danny's imagination. From some unseen source came the rhythmic, nasal whine of Amazigh music, and the air was filled with the heady scent of sand, spices and sun-dried humanity. The people were milling about in a leisurely manner; talking, laughing and conducting business. They wore the traditional long loose-fitting djellaba, the men in white skull caps and the women with coloured headscarves wrapped tightly over their heads. Here was a scene that had changed little in many centuries; the people, the mud-brick buildings and the distant Atlas Mountains shimmering in the heat.

As they left the village, Danny noticed that Angus kept looking in the rear-view mirror. Turning in his seat, he saw a black Mercedes saloon about a hundred metres behind.

'That Merc was behind us when we left Er-Rachida,' said Angus.

'Are you sure it's the same one? There are a lot of Mercedes in this country,' replied Danny.

'True, but they are usually brown, thirty years old, and have a big sign saying 'Taxi' on the top. That one is this year's model, in hoodlum's black, and has smoked-out windows. If ever I've seen a gangster's car, that's it! Hang on, I'm going to try something.'

Angus slowed the Toyota to twenty miles an hour. The black Mercedes slowed as well, keeping the distance between them constant. Angus drove like this for a couple of minutes, then sped up, back to around sixty. The black Mercedes did the same.

'I suppose we should've expected the Sons of Rissouli to keep an eye out for us after last night. But I'd rather they didn't know that we are heading for the well. Then again, they probably don't know that we know what we know.'

Danny thought for a moment. 'Of course, they probably don't know what we know. We know there's a chance that they do know that we know what we know. But we also know that if they *did* know, then they would not have to follow us to find out what we now know, you know?' He looked at Angus and grinned.

'Shut up kid and get out the map.'

Danny, still sniggering, pulled out the map from the box behind his seat and unfolded it.

'Right there's no way we're going to outrun them in this old thing, so we'll have to take roads it can't follow us down,' said Angus. 'Find me a road that goes south over the mountains. The more broken the line is on the map, the rougher the track, which is better for us.'

'There's one here,' Danny said. 'It goes over a pass called… er… Tizi-n'Tazazert and comes out at Nekob.'

Five minutes later, with the black Mercedes still on their tail, they came to a small town and, turning off the main road, threaded their way through the un-signposted streets. Eventually, more by luck than by judgement, they hit the southern fringe of the town and soon found their chosen route.

A dusty trail detached itself from the last of the tarmac and headed off towards the mountains. Soon they were bouncing along a rough corrugated track which stretched across flat stony desert. Their four-wheel drive began to show its advantage. The Mercedes soon slipped behind, struggling with the terrain, and it wasn't long before it was just a black speck trailing a rooster's tail of dust in the distance.

Nevertheless Angus kept his speed up, because there was always a chance that the Sons of Rissouli could arrange to have someone else waiting to meet them when they arrived in Nekob. The sooner they crossed the mountains, the less likely it was there would be a welcoming committee at the other end.

The track got rougher as it began to twist its way up a narrow ravine in the hills, and as the sun reached its zenith high in the African sky, it became unbearably hot. They slowed to a crawl in the difficult conditions as the light breeze, which might normally have had a welcome cooling effect, blew fine dust in through the windows. Danny had never felt so hot in his life. His clothes stuck to him and he itched all over. The dust gave him a raging thirst and cracked his lips.

After what seemed like a century of lurching, bouncing purgatory, the track passed through a jumble of rocky crags and they arrived at the summit of Tizi-n 'Tazazert. They were over seven thousand feet high, with the world spread all around them. A cobalt sky soared above arid mountains and rocky plains, and in the distant south they saw the golden ripple of the sand dunes. At long last

Danny was looking with his own eyes at the incredible vastness of the Sahara.

★ ★ ★

The pass took them over a hundred kilometres of rocky track and Danny wondered how long it would be before the violent vibration would shake the old Toyota to bits. He had visions of it collapsing around them, the doors and wheels falling off, the bonnet popping up and a great geyser of steam shooting out of the radiator. They would be left sitting there with blackened faces, Angus still clutching a steering wheel that had come off in his hands, the parts of the truck scattered around them. Fortunately, however, this didn't happen and it rumbled healthily on, never missing a beat.

By the time they reached Nekob it was late in the afternoon and they were both very glad to get back on to smooth tarmac. They were also relieved to see there was no sign of a welcoming committee and, with new confidence, sped off down the road to Zagora. It was the last settlement on their journey south. After Zagora there were no more petrol stations, no more places to buy food and the only water was at the well they were heading for. A well that could be crawling with gun-running thugs.

South of Zagora, having filled up with diesel, water and a dubious selection of local grub, they found a track which headed roughly in the direction they wanted to go. There were no tracks marked on the map here, it was just a case of picking their way through the desert, heading for the location of the well. Danny had programmed the location into the GPS and watched the direction arrow drift left and right as they struggled to stay on course. To begin with, rocky outcrops and dry river beds caused them to take long diversions, but soon the country flattened out into a featureless plateau.

They drove through the evening light, softened to pink by a haze of Saharan dust suspended like fog in the warm southerly wind. Soon the first long fingers of drifting sand appeared before them, causing the Toyota to roll like a small boat on an ocean swell. A large area of dunes appeared ahead, but these were easily bypassed to the west. The Algerian border passed without any indication of its presence; no signs, no barbed wire, not so much as a line in the sand.

About two kilometres away from the position of the well, they came to a line of dunes that stretched the full length of the horizon. Angus eased the truck to a halt, got out and let the pressure in the tyres down until they were almost flat. He told Danny that the tyres would have extra grip this way. Gunning the engine, he sped at the first dune, hitting it at a good speed. The Toyota raced up the side, slowing as it climbed, until it came almost to a halt on the crest. Angus then pointed the truck straight down the other side and descended slowly, trying not to be too heavy on the brakes in case the wheels locked. The next was taken in the same manner and they continued like this for over a kilometre. They made slow but steady progress until eventually, with the sun touching the horizon, Angus brought the truck to a stop in hollow among some high dunes.

'Right Danny, the well is about five hundred metres that way,' he pointed out of the windscreen in a southerly direction, 'but we'll walk the last bit. If there are any bad guys there I don't want to advertise our presence by rolling up in a noisy old diesel four-wheel drive. We'd better get a move on, it'll be dark soon.'

He jumped out, taking the GPS from its bracket on the dashboard. Danny grabbed a water-bottle and they started off on the last leg of their journey.

★ ★ ★

The GPS was reading eighty seven metres to the position of the well when Danny and Angus plodded up the last dune. However, as soon as they reached the top they both dropped immediately. Beside the well were two black four-wheel drives and, standing nearby, five men.

They peered over the crest to get a better look. Below them, the sand dunes petered out into a flat plain which stretched off to the horizon with just a few dry bushes to break the monotony. Four of the figures that stood by the well were wearing the dark blue hooded djellabas that Danny assumed to be the uniform of the Sons of Rissouli. At their waists hung long curved daggers, or koumyia. The fifth figure was an overweight man in a white shirt and cotton slacks.

As Danny and Angus watched, a dark smudge appeared on the southern horizon. It was clear the men had also seen it, as one of them pointed in its direction and the others nodded their heads in agreement to whatever had been said.

As the minutes passed the smudge got larger and larger until, at last, they could see that it was a cloud of dust thrown up by a vehicle travelling fast over the hard desert. Before long, a travel-stained blue truck skidded to a halt near the well. It was a rough looking vehicle, a smaller version of the type of lorry Danny had seen driving in and out of quarries at home. The driver's door groaned open and out jumped a slim, smartly-dressed man in a black shirt. Shaking hands with the fat man, the pair began talking earnestly, their heads inches apart like schoolboys sharing a secret. Meanwhile, the others started transferring long, heavy-looking crates from the back of his truck over to the two four-wheel drives.

'This is what we've been waiting for, Danny. Those are standard small arms crates. I've seen them before, I'd recognise them anywhere.' Angus's voice quivered with excitement. 'And I'll bet you dollars to donuts they're full of Brunton hardware.'

By the time the men had loaded all the crates, the sun had set, revealing stars glittering in a sky of blue velvet. The smugglers squatted in the light of a paraffin lamp to talk and drink tea. Angus was trying to decide which of the vehicles they should follow when the fat man stood up and said something to the others. The men laughed and the fat man started walking directly towards Danny and Angus.

'What the hell's he doing?' whispered Danny, alarmed.

'Shut up and lie completely still. He might not have seen

us in the dark.'

Danny lay as still as the dead, flat against the warm sand, as the man approached. All he could hear was the dull thump of his heart against his own ribs and the sand squeaking under the fat man's feet. He dared not breathe and dug his fingers into the sand, wishing he could sink beneath the surface and hide there until the danger had passed.

The fat man came closer and closer, heading directly for them. Then, when he was just a few paces away, his purpose became apparent. In the soft, white light of the stars they could make out that he was unbuttoning his fly.

Just as he was about to relieve himself, he spotted them. For a long moment they all froze, each of them wondering what to do next. Realising the game was up, Angus grinned, his teeth gleaming white in the starlight. 'Good evening. Could you point us in the direction of the nearest arms dealer? We'd like to purchase a machine gun.'

The man stared, his mouth opening and shutting like a goldfish's, as though he was trying to form words but his brain wasn't quite up to the task. Then he did something quite unexpected: he screamed. A shrill, warbling scream that sounded quite unlikely coming from a man of his bulk. He turned and stumbled off down the dune, shouting to his associates. Having already unbuttoned his fly, he only managed five steps before his trousers fell to his ankles and he tripped. Danny stared as the screaming smuggler tumbled in a chaotic mass of whirling limbs and flapping clothing to the foot of the dune.

'Move! Come on, run. RUN, YOU PLONKER!' Angus shouted, pulling him to his feet. From the well, came the clamour of sudden action as the smugglers realised what was happening. Angus and Danny ran, throwing themselves down the dune in a landslide. Soon they were struggling slowly up the side of another and Danny realised it would be a miracle if they escaped. It was painfully slow going in the soft sand and even though they were running as fast as they could, it would take a long time to climb each dune. The next moment they heard a heart-stopping sound, the repeated thumping crack of a machine gun.

'Sweet merciful crap!' shouted Danny, as he felt the slipstream of a bullets tear past his cheek, 'They've got guns!'

'No! *Really?*' panted Angus, managing to inject more than a little sarcasm into the words. 'What an odd thing for gun-runners to be carrying around!'

'Very funny,' panted Danny, 'but we don't. What are we going to do?'

'There's only one thing we can do...'

From the direction of the well came the cough and rumble of an engine starting up. As Danny and Angus scrambled through the night they could hear revving as the vehicle sped up into the dunes. Suddenly the darkness was obliterated by an explosion of white light behind them. They were caught in the headlights. They froze momentarily, blinded by the light, unsure where to run. There was shouting and the flash and crack of the machine gun. The sand around them erupted as bullets ploughed into it.

'RUN! RUN LIKE HELL!'

And they were off again. Following Angus's example, Danny ducked and weaved to throw off their pursuers' aim. As they ran, hell for leather, the twin beams lost them and they disappeared. Seconds later they topped a dune as the headlights picked them up again, trapping them in a terrible brightness and exposing them to the aim of the machine gunner. Bullets tore into the sand around them and they jinked and turned, like rabbits evading a fox. Then suddenly, the smugglers lost them to the night again and Danny and Angus ran on into the darkness. Somewhere behind them the Sons of Rissouli were emptying bullets into anything and everything. In the distance Danny and Angus could see the glow of the headlights sweeping the dunes and the staccato flashes and bangs of the machine gun fire. They ran on, not daring to stop and rest.

'If they find us again,' Angus said, 'we'll split up. Hopefully that'll confuse them long enough for both of us to escape. I'll meet you back at the Toyota.'

'That doesn't sound like much of a plan,' replied Danny.

'No, but unless you can think of something better...?' At that moment there was a sudden roar of an engine and the Sons of Rissouli appeared over a dune to their right. More shouting and a cacophony of noise as the machine gun again spewed bullets into the night towards Danny and Angus.

'GO!' yelled Angus, pointing to their left, and Danny went off, running as fast as he could. The last he saw of Angus was a running figure caught in a circle of white light, with geysers of sand spouting up around him. Behind him raced the menacing bulk of the smugglers' four-wheel drive, with a dark figure hanging out of a window, silhouetted by the bright flashes from the gun he held in his hands.

★ ★ ★

Angus accelerated into a hard sprint. Danny could run quite fast for a lad of his age, but Angus would normally have run much faster. Now that Danny was safely headed off and the Sons of Rissouli were chasing him alone, Angus knew he could really put the speed on. Without the burden of looking after Danny, he also began to think more clearly. On their hike from the hollow where they had left the Toyota, they had trudged over a succession of dunes. Some were low and rose in gentle ripples like waves on a calm sea, while others rose steeply like miniature mountains, with sharp ridges and steep sides. Remembering that one dune had a gentle southern slope and a steep drop to the north, Angus quickly hit upon a plan.

The smugglers were gaining fast, less than two hundred metres behind him now, he guessed. The dunes had become smaller and more rolling, making it harder for Angus to hide behind them and easier for the vehicle to speed up. Another burst of gunfire tore up the sand around him. The next fifty metres were critical; if he could make it to the top of the dune his plan might just work. With the muscles in his legs burning from the exertion and his breathing coming in painful gasps, he charged up the final slopes. He could hear the four-wheel drive bearing down on him, the scream of its engine roaring in his ears. It seemed as though the rest of the world had disappeared into the night. All that existed was his aching body, those final few metres of sand dune and the roaring behemoth poised to crush him. The smugglers were so close he could hear them yelling and the slide of the machine gun clacking back each time it was fired. Angus could not believe they hadn't hit him yet, they must have fired off hundreds of rounds. But he knew his luck could not last: it was only a matter of seconds before they were too close to miss.

When at last he reached the crest of the dune, he threw himself headlong over the edge into the unknown below. For a moment he was falling through the air and everything became strangely quiet. Then he crashed into the other side and started tumbling through the sliding sands, out of control, down into the blackness.

A couple of seconds afterwards, the smugglers' four-wheel drive followed above him, still speeding and with its machine gunner leaning out of the window firing wildly into the night. By the time its driver had realised the dune had a drop behind it, it was too late. Their wheels were already spinning over the edge - with nothing but a dark, empty void below them.

As Angus rolled to a stop in a shallow at the foot of the dune he looked up and saw the flying vehicle silhouetted against the stars. Then, as the front of it dropped, he blinked in the glare of the headlights. The burning white orbs dipped, then bounced, dipped again and then inexplicably disappeared into the darkness. A split second later Angus realised why, as a pair of red lights suddenly swooped into view, followed by a sickening, squealing crash. The truck had flipped and was now somersaulting down the dune towards him.

In one final, exhausted effort, Angus lunged up from his kneeling position and dived as far to his right as he could. He knew he had only thrown himself a couple of feet, but it was enough. The truck smashed, roof down, with an ear-splitting bang, just inches from his feet. He covered his head with his hands as a shower of broken glass from the windows exploded over him and then he lay still in the heavy silence that followed.

Slowly, he raised his head and stared at the twisted remains beside him. The headlights still shone into the dunes ahead, making the tiny fragments of glass glisten like a million diamonds, but all else lay in shattered silence. Shards of plastic and chunks of trim were scattered around the vehicle, and lying several yards away was the spare wheel. Angus took a deep breath and tried to peer inside the passenger compartment. The roof had collapsed leaving only a thin gap where the windows had once been. Inside, he could just about make out the lifeless bodies of the smugglers. There was no way anyone could have survived in such a mangled wreck of twisted steel. Walking round to the other side he came upon a gruesome sight. Lying half out of the passenger window was the bloodied torso of the machine gunner. He was still gripping the machine gun, which trailed a long belt of ammunition. The man must have been hanging out of the window as they went over the edge, and had still been hanging out as the truck had tumbled over and over until it had landed squarely upon its roof. The roof had compacted completely on his side, not stopping till it had come into contact with the top of the door. The machine gunner, so keen to end the lives of Danny and Angus, had been sliced in two, as cleanly as though by a giant pair of scissors.

Angus looked away, feeling suddenly dizzy. He took a few deep breaths, fighting the desire to collapse to his knees and be sick. A few moments later he straightened and, without looking back, started limping north, back to where his Toyota was waiting.

CHAPTER FOUR

After watching Angus disappear into the dunes, swiftly followed by the smugglers, Danny ran on into the darkness. For a while he could still hear the roar of the engine and the crackle of machine gun fire. Occasionally he got a glimpse of reflected light from the headlights as they swept over a distant dune. It was not long, however, before the noise faded to nothing, leaving no hint as to where the chase might be heading.

Becoming increasingly exhausted, he staggered on through the dunes in the direction of the Toyota. It seemed much further away than he had expected, and he was starting to get worried. Deciding it would be a good idea to get his bearings before he blundered off course into the middle of the Sahara, Danny climbed to the top of a high dune, and sat down at the top. He was surprised at how far he could see in the starlight. In all directions, the silver dunes rolled off, seemingly into infinity, under a sky shining with more stars than Danny had ever seen in his life. There were so many that it would have been difficult to find space for any more. Although there was no moon, it was light enough for Danny to read the numbers on his watch without difficulty.

As he looked around, he realised that he could easily have veered wildly off course. These sand dunes all looked the same and he now had no idea where the Toyota lay hidden.

With a feeling of rising panic, he searched the landscape for some recognisable feature, some insignificant indicator of where he might be. Staring out desperately into the darkness, he was gripped by a tight, sick sensation in his stomach. He truly had no idea where he was or in which direction he should be heading. The endless desert was becoming a very menacing place. He fought hard to suppress the terror that seized him.

'Keep calm!' he told himself, saying the words aloud. *What would Uncle Angus do in this situation?* he wondered. But he could not come up with the answer. He had never felt so hopeless, so alone, and so completely out of his depth.

He started to shiver. The temperature had dropped sharply since the sun had gone down and he was thirsty and had no water, having dropped the bottle during the escape. He had lost his uncle and there were murderous smugglers chasing him. No, he had certainly had better days. He wondered what his fate would be. Would he be found and shot? Would he freeze to death in the bitter desert night? Or would he survive until morning, simply to die of a raging thirst under the broiling Saharan sun? He decided the first would be the easiest way to go; at least it would be quick. Danny laughed softly to himself; a fortnight ago he would never have believed being gunned down in a hail of bullets could be seen as a favourable outcome.

He wondered what his friends were doing back in Scotland. Lying in their own beds presumably, fast asleep and safe from the world. Dreaming about what? Colin would be dreaming about girls, Danny had not much doubt about that, the mucky sod. Either that or being lead guitarist in an indie band. Evan? Well, assuming he wasn't dreaming about girls too (which was a distinct possibility) he would be dreaming about adventure. Yes, Evan's dreams would probably have him summiting some savage Himalayan peak, hacking his way through primordial jungle, or, it was entirely feasible, on the run from gun-runners in the Sahara...

Danny smiled. He had dreamt about being involved in adventures like this for as long as he could remember. He was sure Evan would give his eye teeth to swap places with him right now. With this thought Danny felt a little better. If, by some miracle, he survived this ridiculous situation, he would be the envy of his friends for years to come. It didn't matter what tricks Evan could pull off a table-top on his jump bike, or that Colin could play like Jimi Hendrix and looked like Tobey Maguire. Danny had been chased by actual gun-runners through the Sahara desert! None of them would ever be able to top that!

With his mood suddenly lightened he began to look more appreciatively at the stars. They really were incredible out here. In the city, the light that shone from people's homes and shops, from streetlamps and car headlights, polluted the atmosphere with a reflected glow that made it difficult to see the stars. Out here there was no such light pollution and they sparkled and twinkled in their vast multitudes. To his right a shooting star traced the heavens in a fleeting streak and he turned his head to follow it. As it faded, he recognised some groups of stars close by: Orion, standing out so boldly in the sky, still waving his sword as he had that distant night by an orange grove in Spain. It was one of the two constellations he could recognise...

One of the two constellations he could recognise!

Danny leapt to his feet with a rush of excitement. If he could only find the other one... And there it was, just on the other side of the Milky Way: the Plough!

He could have kicked himself for not thinking of it earlier. After all, if you can find the Plough in the night sky, you can find the Pole Star and, as everyone knows, find the Pole Star and you have found the North! Danny had always wondered why it was called the Plough, as it looked more like a saucepan to him. Whatever it looked like, he knew that the two stars at the end of the Plough pointed to the Pole Star. He chuckled to himself, this was almost too cool for words. Not only had he been chased through the Sahara by smugglers, he was about to navigate his way out of trouble using the stars!

He and Angus had headed due south from where they had parked to find the well, so Danny now headed straight for the Pole Star. By heading due north, he should pass close enough to the Toyota to find it in the starlight.

He had only taken a few paces, however, when he heard something that made his gut tighten. It was the throaty growl of an engine, and he was pretty sure it wasn't the Toyota. The noise was getting rapidly louder and he realised that the vehicle that was making it could not be far away. Quickening, he kept his eyes fixed on the Pole Star and hurried on.

As he strode on into the night, the noise got louder and louder. Occasionally light would sweep briefly across a nearby dune. The vehicle, whatever it was, was getting too close for comfort and Danny broke into a run. He turned in fear as bright lights suddenly appeared over a dune behind him and shouts joined in the roaring of the engine. How the hell had they found him? Well, it didn't matter now, what mattered was making sure they lost him again. He ducked out of the glare of the headlights and sprinted off. He leapt over the top of a dune and ran along the depression behind it, but a few seconds later the lights appeared behind him again. As he started the slow exhausting run up the next dune he realised that no matter how fast he ran, he would never out-pace the four-wheel drive, which was now just a few yards behind him.

Dropping to his knees he threw up his hands in surrender. Closing his eyes he waited for the bullets to rip into him. He hoped it would not hurt too much, hoped it would be the kind of instant, bloodless death of old cowboy movies.

To his surprise, the bullets never came. The vehicle roared to a halt behind him and shouting figures leapt out. Before there was time to react he had been knocked to the ground and his face pushed hard into the sand. He felt blows on his ribs as someone kicked him repeatedly and then a sharp pain on the back of his head. The world spun wildly for a moment and he tried to raise himself, then everything went black as he fell into oblivion.

★ ★ ★

Danny regained consciousness slowly. He became aware of a pounding pain in the back of his skull, then as he opened his eyes, the glare of the early morning sun seared into his eyeballs, intensifying the pain in his head. His whole body ached like he had been…well, beaten senseless by a gang of thugs. As the world slowly swam into focus, he looked around. Not far away stood four men, drinking mint tea in the morning sun. Behind them were two vehicles: a black four-wheel drive and a blue truck.

Danny had been bound hand and foot with zip ties. When he realised that struggling against them merely made them tighter, he stopped. Before long one of the men turned to look at him and noticed he had woken up. It was the tall, slim man in the black shirt who had arrived at the well in the blue truck the previous evening. He immediately strode over, his face dark and twisted with anger. 'Ah, t'es réveillé toi? Ordure! Qui es-tu et qu'est-ce qui est arrivé à mes hommes? Je devrais t'étriper immédiatement comme un cochon!'

Danny recoiled in fear, he recognised the language being spoken, it was French, but he had no idea what was being said, only that the man's tone was threatening, aggressive.

'I…I'm sorry, I don't understand,' he stammered. The black shirted thug's face was an inch from his own, the cloying stench of mint tea and tobacco on his hot breath made Danny feel suddenly sick.

'Ah!' the thug straightened, 'You are English. Which, of course, means you speak only your own language! Abruti!' He swung a vicious kick at Danny, hitting him squarely in the stomach. He grunted, fighting to stay conscious as the pain made his head swim and vision darken.

'WHAT HAPPENED TO MY MEN?' he screamed. He was holding Danny by the throat now, his bloodshot eyes staring in wild rage. 'WHAT…' he was breathing hard, flecks of spittle on his lips, he looked as though his head might just explode at any moment. Abruptly his breathing slowed and the hand around Danny's throat relaxed a little. In a voice barely above a whisper he hissed '…did you do to them?'

'I have no idea what you are talking about!' pleaded Danny, terrified. He would have to think fast if he was going to talk his way out of this one. 'My uncle and I are here on holiday, honestly... We're just driving through the desert.'

It wasn't the most watertight excuse for being near the well, but it was all Danny could think of on the spur of the moment, and he knew if he admitted the truth he risked being murdered out of hand. 'It's quite good fun...' he offered, realising belatedly that this might seem like an odd thing to say, given his current predicament. The thug looked at him suspiciously, as though he might just be entertaining the possibility that Danny was telling the truth.

'Do you know who I am?' he asked, and then, without waiting for a reply, continued: 'My name is Khalid Rissouli and I am the most dangerous man in Morocco. Lie to me and I will kill you in the most unpleasant way. For you…ah, yes, I think I would tie you to the ground and paint your face with honey. It would not be long before the ants found you. They eat the eyes first you know, then climb into your nose and eat your brain from the inside…and yet…' he sighed regretfully '…it would still take three days for you to die.'

Danny studied Khalid's face, trying to determine the man behind the scowl. He was good looking, in an effete sort of a way, with regular aquiline features and dark coiffured hair. He looked arrogant and proud. Danny decided that his words were not idle threats; if he was going to lie, he had better be damn convincing.

'Honestly, we were just driving through the desert when we ran out of water. We saw a well on the map and decided to investigate. We left the car nearby in case there was any wildlife near the well…you know, in case the noise of the engine scared it off… I'm really hoping to see a Fennec fox.'

Danny was pretty pleased with this. Not bad for off-the-cuff deceit, he thought to himself, hoping it would be enough to convince Khalid not to kill him.

Khalid removed his hand from Danny's throat and stood up. Danny thought that he seemed unsure of what to do next; maybe he stood a chance of surviving this after all.

'Really? Fascinating. I will not argue this with you now. What I really want to know is how two of my men come to be lying dead under their car and your uncle, despite our best efforts, seems to have vanished…pof!' he snapped his fingers, '…into thin air?'

Danny had to fight hard to suppress a grin. So Angus had got away... Suddenly he felt a surge of hope, certain his uncle would do everything in his power to rescue him.

'I'm sorry,' he said, 'I really don't know what happened to your men.' This, at least, *was* true. Danny genuinely had no idea what had happened to them. 'Like I said…'

'Yes, yes, I know. You were driving around the desert looking for foxes!' There was heavy sarcasm in Khalid's voice. 'I do not have time to play games just now.'

He gestured to his men and without a word they advanced on Danny, slipping a hood of dark material over his head. Danny felt himself being grabbed roughly by the arms and legs, and lifted up in to the air. A few seconds later he was dumped onto a hard, ridged surface. It felt like the floor in the back of a vehicle.

★ ★ ★

As the night wore on, Angus became more and more concerned about Danny. He sat on the top of a high dune near the truck and kept lookout. From there he could see a long way in the starlight but there was no sign of his nephew. They had parked less than half a kilometre from the well. Surely he could not have got lost? On the other hand, Angus knew that sand dunes were notoriously easy to get lost in.

At around midnight Angus had seen the lights of a vehicle

to the west, but after that nothing had disturbed the cold desert night. Although sick with worry, he knew there was nothing he could do but wait. To wander about the desert aimlessly shouting Danny's name was to invite discovery by the smugglers, and he was no more likely to find him than if he just stayed put. At least up here he could scan the horizon in all directions, searching for some sign of the missing boy.

Eventually, after a night that seemed to last a hundred years, the first light of dawn began to fade the stars in the east. As the sun rose higher in the sky, the temperature rose with it, and soon it was uncomfortably hot. By nine o'clock Danny had still not turned up and Angus decided he must do something; he simply could not bear to just sit and wait any longer. Raising himself wearily from the sand, he started to head south, back to the well. Perhaps the smugglers had found Danny, and perhaps they hadn't simply murdered him, but were keeping him alive for some reason. If this was the case it might be possible to rescue him, or at least barter for his release. Angus realised this really was his only hope. Because if not, and Danny had become lost among the sand dunes, Angus knew he would be lucky to last more than a couple of days before he died of thirst.

Before long he was back at the spot where they had been discovered the night before, crouching near the top of a sand dune, staring down at the well a short distance away. This time, there was only one vehicle by the well. There was no sign of the blue truck. Next to the four-wheel drive, clearing away a paraffin stove and some glasses, were the fat man who'd raised the alarm the previous night and one of the thugs dressed in a blue djellaba.

Lying in the sand, Angus strained to hear what was being said, to get some clue as to what had happened the night before. He caught snatches of conversation borne on the light morning breeze. As they were speaking French, presumably the fat man was not Amazigh and this was their common language.

Clearly discussing the journey ahead of them, he heard: '…Mon Dieu. Il fait chaud ! Allons-y…' ('My God, it's hot! Let's get going…') then, 'Partons au nord par l'intermédiaire de Merzouga…' ('Partons au nord par Merzouga…') For a few seconds Angus could hear nothing when the breeze blew in the wrong direction, but then he heard something that made his heart stop. 'Incitera le garçon à parler, vous verrez…' ('Will make the boy talk, you'll see…')

So they did have Danny! That could be the only explanation for the comment. But there was no sign of him here. Angus had a reasonable view of the inside of their car, and could see nothing but munitions crates stacked almost to the roof in both the boot and back seat. The loss of the other vehicle the night before meant the smugglers were having to cram every inch of this one with the load from the other. There was certainly no room for hostages in there, he thought. Danny must be in the blue truck, wherever that was.

Angus scanned the horizon as best he could. The desert wind

had strengthened now, whipping up a haze of dust that blotted out the horizon. Visibility had already shortened to less than a few kilometres and flurries of sand were washing up towards the dunes where Angus was hiding. There was no way of telling which direction the blue truck might have taken; although the chances were it had returned south. Angus had no doubt that once the four-wheel drive had been loaded it would head north, in order to deliver the weapons to their destination.

The two men by the well were hurrying now, shooting nervous glances to the South-East, where the sky had turned a dirty brown and the morning sun had gone the colour of molten iron. Angus knew what this meant: there was a sandstorm on the way. He had to act fast if he was not to lose these two. Had he not been certain they had handguns, he would have risked charging them there and then, forcing them to tell him where Danny had been taken. But trying that with armed men would simply get him shot. He would just have to follow them for now and see if an opportunity arose to take them by surprise.

Turning away, he started to head back to the Toyota. As he did, a car door slammed shut behind him. They would be leaving soon – there was no time to lose. He broke into a run, but the soft sand slowed him down. He scrambled back without stopping to catch his breath, leapt straight into the cab, and started the engine.

He reckoned if he followed the obvious route north-east to Merzouga he might be able to catch them up. They would probably not hang about – not with a vehicle full of contraband weapons – but with no idea they were being chased they would not be in a hurry either.

With the clear memory of the mangled heap of the other vehicle that had chased him the night before, he approached each dune with caution, only speeding up when he could see clearly what lay ahead. It was frustratingly slow progress but he took comfort from knowing that the smugglers would not be travelling any faster. Soon the dunes started to lose some height and became shallower and more rolling, giving Angus a better view of the route ahead. He opened up the throttle accordingly. Driving like a competitor in the Paris-Dakar Rally, he blasted over the dunes. The Toyota regularly left the ground completely, its engine screaming as all four wheels spun in the air. It would come to earth with a shattering crash, a ton and a half of machine and equipment bouncing wildly for a few seconds with Angus fighting for control.

As he roared on, the sky darkened and the sandstorm closed in. It was as though a thin orange-brown mist had enveloped the world, blotting out the horizon. The visibility was dropping fast and Angus worried that he would not be able to find his quarry. The wind had picked up, throwing flurries of sand from the tops of the dunes and buffeting the truck in moaning gusts. It was stiflingly hot in the cab and the finest windblown sand had got in through the air vents and hung suspended in the air, coating everything with a layer of dust.

He had been driving for about an hour when the dunes began to peter away altogether. Now they were just occasional long, low banks snaking across areas of harder ground. Here, the desert was strewn with small black rocks which rattled off the bottom of the car with loud thumps and bangs as it bounced along over them. With the dunes finally disappearing, the landscape opened out and despite the rapidly failing light, Angus could see much further than before. Suddenly, to his great excitement, he spotted a vehicle about a kilometre ahead, and as he gained on it, he saw that it was indeed the smugglers.

It was at this moment that the sandstorm hit with all its ferocity. A violent gust of wind lashed the Toyota, causing it to shudder along its length. The sun was blotted out and the world was cast into an ominous gloom, like the polluted twilight of an industrial city. He could barely see thirty metres ahead and the black four-wheel drive had vanished into the swirling sands.

'Goddammit,' Angus growled. 'Typical!'

He pulled the GPS from his pocket, clipped it into its bracket on the dashboard and set it to compass mode. If nothing else, he could continue following a bearing that would take him in generally the right direction. A quick look at the map and he decided upon a bearing of 40 degrees. A pretty rough estimate, but close enough to the right direction as would make no difference. The chances of seeing the smugglers again were so slim it was barely worth continuing the pursuit, but he carried on regardless. While there was still any chance of finding out where Danny had been taken, he must continue the chase, no matter what the odds against success.

The driving had become insanely dangerous. Obstacles reared abruptly out of the sandstorm giving him just fractions of a second to react. Angus steered violently around boulders, bushes, even the rotting corpse of a camel, the car rolling sickeningly with each sudden yank on the steering wheel. After nearly crashing into an outcrop of rock, he eased the pace a little, realising he was gambling with disaster.

The sandstorm howled through the landscape like a banshee, unstoppable in its fury. It seemed to have torn the desert from the earth, hurling it about in a choking rage. Angus drove on, as fast as he dared and much faster than was sensible, following the bearing on the GPS. The noise in the cab was deafening: savage hisses of sand waves breaking on the bodywork, the roar of the engine and the clattering of the rocks being thrown up by the wheels.

All Angus could see ahead was twenty metres of desert and a dense brown blanket of airborne granules. Then suddenly, looming out of the murk, came the back end of the smugglers' car. It came and went in a tantalising moment, like a ghost ship rearing out of the mist. As it disappeared back into the dust, Angus pushed his foot down on the accelerator. He knew they were just yards ahead, hidden somewhere in the maelstrom.

For fifteen tense seconds he saw nothing. Then it appeared again, its brake lights flickering as the driver slowed to avoid some obstacle. Angus was gaining fast and knew he must make a snap decision. There seemed to be only one thing he could do, so he floored the accelerator. A split second later

Angus was ploughing into the side of the other car, just behind the front wheel. There was a sickening bang, followed by the squealing of metal tearing into metal. Both cars' side windows exploded in a shower of glass. Angus smashed the bridge of his nose on the steering wheel, and recoiling saw the heads of the fat man and his friend snap round in shock, just before their vehicle started to roll. It pitched onto two wheels, where it seemed to hang for a long moment on a point of balance. Then it began to tip further, slowly at first, finally rolling in a sudden flip. There was another hideous bang as it landed on its roof, and (to Angus's surprise) continued to roll. Like a huge, deformed black beach ball it bounced across the rocky desert, at last coming to rest the right way up: wheels down, roof skyward.

It took a few seconds for Angus to recover from the shock of the collision. In a daze he lifted his hand to his face and it came away smeared with blood. Shaking his head to clear his thoughts, he remembered gradually what he was meant to be doing. 'Come on, you idiot, get going!' he snarled at himself, climbing from the car and starting in the direction of the smugglers.

As he strode over, their right passenger door creaked open and the fat man fell out, landing in a heap on the ground. He quickly recovered and started off in a staggering run. The stunned driver was wiping blood from what looked like a broken nose. Looking up, he saw Angus and, with an expression of furious hatred, reached into the folds of his djellaba. Angus knew instinctively what he was doing and broke into a desperate sprint towards him. He was only a few metres away when he saw the gun, a menacing lump of angular metal in the smuggler's hand. The thug was struggling with the slide, trying to get the gun cocked and ready to fire. It clicked back, clacked forward. In what seemed like slow motion he turned and brought the gun level.

He almost made it. He almost had the gun at Angus's chest. Almost blew a hole the size of a cricket ball through him. But Angus was just a fraction of a second too fast, swinging a hard right hook through the broken window as he reached the car. It was a fine punch, connecting squarely with the side of the chin. And it was enough to knock the already dazed smuggler insensible. The handgun dropped harmlessly to the sand at Angus's feet.

He snatched it up and started after the other criminal before he disappeared completely into the sandstorm. The fat man had clearly been hurt. He was staggering across the desert in a zig-zag. Angus barely had to break into a jog to catch up. With a single-handed shove, he pushed him to the ground.

He lay on his back moaning, his breaths coming in rapid gasps. Angus stood over him, pointing the gun at his head. He had to speak loudly over the noise of the wind: 'Where have they taken my boy?' The smuggler simply groaned, turned away from the wind and covered his head with his hands.

'Hey!' Angus lashed out hard with his foot. 'WHERE THE HELL IS THE BOY?'

'To hell with you!' shouted the smuggler through the pain. 'If I tell you anything, I will be murdered!'

Angus dropped to his knees, and grabbed the smuggler by his flabby throat. It was horribly greasy with sweat and blood and gritty with windblown sand. Leaning forward he stared menacingly into the fat man's eyes. He pushed the barrel of the handgun hard into his ample belly and shouted, 'If you don't tell me where they have taken the boy, I will open your stomach over the desert. How long do you suppose it will take you to die?'

For a moment the two men glared at each other, one trying to look like he meant what he said, and the other's nerve slowly crumbling. Angus jabbed the gun in a little harder. It worked. Choosing a short reprieve from the certainty of death, the smuggler blurted out, 'OKAY! OKAY! Mon Dieu, do not kill me! They may have taken the boy to Dakar in Senegal.'

'"MAY?"' yelled Angus. 'Let me tell you something, "*May*" is not good enough. "*May*" gets you a bullet in the guts!'

'I'm sorry! Please! I know nothing! Khalid tells me nothing!'

Angus stared into his eyes. He could see fear and hatred in them, but no sign of duplicity. He was clearly too scared to consider lying.

'OK, so where in Dakar? It's a big city, I need an address.' He thrust the gun in harder, as a reminder of what would happen if he hesitated.

'STOP!' the smuggler spluttered, tears welling in his eyes. 'Do not kill me! I will tell you!'

Angus suddenly felt a little sorry for him; he could not know that Angus was no more likely to shoot him in the stomach than kiss him on the mouth.

The instinct of self-preservation had made the man talkative, and he gave Angus an address in the dockyard area in the north-east of Dakar. It was a warehouse, he said, where they stored weapons for export. However, the Sons of Rissouli's living quarters were in a villa on the Route de la Corniche-Ouest, overlooking the Atlantic Ocean. The villa was their base of all operations, but Danny was more likely to be taken to the warehouse to keep him out of the way. Angus realised grimly that it would also be easier to dispose of a body in a quiet shipyard at night than it would be in a residential neighbourhood. He hoped he could reach Danny in time, but it was a long way to Dakar. He would have to cross back into Morocco and then travel south through Mauritania in order to reach Senegal.

There was no point in hanging around; Angus stood up, turned on his heel and ran back to the Toyota.

CHAPTER FIVE

It was not going to be a comfortable journey – that much was obvious. Smothered in the darkness of a hood, Danny could not see a thing. But his other senses were suffering a shattering assault. The zip-ties on his wrists and ankles bit into his flesh remorselessly as the ridges in the floor slammed his hip and shoulder with every bump.

The truck, an ageing behemoth that looked like it had been cobbled together with old fence-posts and recycled farm machinery, rattled and roared along in a bellowing cacophony of noise which made Danny's ears ring. Pervading this dark, painful world was the cloying stench of oil and diesel.

After a while, the truck slowed. Danny did not care why; he was grateful for anything that eased the horrendous pounding his body was taking. The engine noise lessened and then stopped altogether as the truck came to a halt. Listening carefully, Danny became aware of a hissing noise, then a moaning howl which, he thought, sounded like a strong wind blowing through cracks in a wall.

A smell, curiously like that of burning toast, joined the reek of diesel, and as it grew unbearably hot, Danny's lips and throat became dry and sore. He tried to swallow but could not. He started to feel as though he was suffocating in the black constriction of the hood, and felt a sudden rush of claustrophobia. His heart pounded in his chest and he fought for breath. Somewhere in the back of his mind a little voice told him to lie still, to relax, that panicking was the worst thing he could do. But he could not help himself. He struggled in terror, thrashing his arms and legs in an attempt to loosen the grip of the zip-ties.

Then he stopped, freezing abruptly as a horrific realisation swept over him. The smell of burning, the heat, the curious noises, the choking atmosphere… it could mean only one thing: they had set fire to the truck with him inside!

At that moment the panic was complete; losing all composure he started shouting and struggling with all his might.

'HELP! HELP! DON'T BURN ME! I CAN TELL YOU THINGS…IMPORTANT THINGS!'

Danny was desperate now, would say anything to save his life. He knew he must convince them that it was worth keeping him alive, that he had some information which could be useful to them. It was getting hotter with every second and his head throbbed with pain. The sweat poured out of him and he choked and coughed between painful gasps for air. He was just gathering breath for a second bout of yelling when there was an unexpected sound. A loud 'clunk' echoed through the truck, followed by the creaking of an iron hinge.

'Shut up, you stupid pig!'

The truck rocked from side to side as approaching footsteps thumped across the metal floor. There was a brief moment of silence, before the hood was suddenly pulled off. Standing over him was a dark, angry figure. It was Khalid, the black-shirted thug, covered with a dusting of sand. Danny looked past him. There was no sign of flames or smoke, just a powerful wind battering the sides of the truck and churning the desert sands into a swirling brown fog.

'What is the problem?' Khalid shouted over the noise of the wind. 'Believe me, my friend, I am this close…' he held his forefinger and thumb a few millimetres apart, 'to shooting you in the guts. It would be in your best interests not to trouble me further!'

'Sorry!' Danny gasped, 'I thought…I'm sorry, I thought…' he paused. There was no point in telling Khalid that he had imagined he was being burned alive, it might give him ideas. 'I thought I was dying of thirst. Can I have a drink?'

Khalid nodded and left through the tailgate. For a few precious moments Danny was left alone without his hood. He looked around frantically for anything that might help him escape, but there was nothing. He could see the truck was very roughly made and had evidently survived a long and tough life. It looked like it had been repaired many times, with a metal floor that had been crudely welded in several places and wooden sides that were patched with new plywood. Light filtered in through the numerous cracks, but there were no windows and the tailgate appeared to be secured with a heavy bolt. At that moment, it swung open and Khalid reappeared with a bottle of water which he uncapped, pouring half the contents down Danny's throat.

'Thank you.' Danny spluttered, and he meant it. He hadn't had a drink since the night before and his lips were parched and his tongue swollen. 'Why have we stopped?' he asked, with a dreadful feeling that the smugglers might have pulled up somewhere nice and remote in order to shoot him. Maybe the gulp of water he had just been given was equivalent to the last cigarette of a condemned man... He was mightily relieved when Khalid told him the actual reason.

'You don't know?' He seemed genuinely surprised. 'There is a sandstorm. It is far too dangerous to carry on. This part of the desert has many oueds and hidden ravines. In this, ah… visibilité, we could crash in the bottom of one before we knew it was there.'

'Where are you taking me? What are you going to do to me?' Danny did not quite manage to keep the nervousness from his voice.

At this, Khalid grinned maliciously. 'You will find out soon enough,' he said and then bent down, pulling the hood over his head again. Danny listened to the sound of his retreating footsteps, the creak of the tailgate being opened and a slight wobble as the smuggler jumped to the ground. Danny wondered what Khalid had meant by his last comment and was disturbed by the sinister way he had smiled at him. He made up his mind that if the slightest opportunity arose to escape, he would jump at it. Little did he realise how far he would have to jump...

★ ★ ★

The next three days rumbled painfully by. Danny managed

to drag himself into a seated position against the side of the truck, which was only slightly less uncomfortable than lying on the floor. The heat and dust continued in an almost unbearable purgatory. Sweat soaked his shirt, making him itch all over. He felt filthy and dehydrated, and vaguely wondered why he had not yet been killed and for what purpose they were keeping him alive.

He heard many different noises while smothered in the confines of the hood. There was the soft hiss of sand as they rolled over dunes and the rattling drum of the wheels on hard, corrugated tracks. Occasionally a loud, ringing clang would indicate a rock being thrown up by the wheels against the underside of the truck and, of course, there was the constant phlegmy rumble of the prehistoric diesel engine. But not once did he hear the sounds of people on their long journey through the desert, no voices or music, not even the swishing rumble of other traffic. They must be travelling by quiet tracks indeed. Not once did they seem to stop at a junction or pass through the smallest village. Danny knew that wherever they were, it was the middle of nowhere.

★ ★ ★

Once a day one of the smugglers would open the back of the truck and come in. Removing his hood and cutting the zip-ties from his hands they would give him a loaf of flatbread and a bottle of water. Danny would wolf these down, well aware that this would be the only sustenance he would get that day.

When he had finished he would be let out of the truck to go to the toilet.

This was Danny's only chance to see the country through which they were passing. It was unremittingly forbidding. They appeared to be heading right into the heart of the Sahara, and the desert, as though enraged by the violation of their presence, seemed to be trying to cook them alive for the transgression. After being kept under the hood, the daylight was blinding and the scorching heat of the direct sun made him feel faint. All Danny could see was a flat plateau, broken by the occasional dark scar of broken cliffs. On the second day, he spotted some mountains in the distance, rising like the shattered remains of an ancient city from the surrounding desert. It was clear that to try to escape out here was to invite certain death. With nowhere to escape to he would have to wait for a more appropriate time.

At around noon on the fourth day, the truck eased slowly to a halt. As usual, Danny heard the squealing creak of the tailgate opening, followed by approaching footsteps. And as usual, Danny was starving and his throat was dry and sore. His tongue felt twice its normal size and kept sticking to the top of his mouth. The hood was pulled off his head and Khalid dropped a loaf of bread and a bottle of water in his lap before bending down to cut the ties around his wrists.

'Thank you,' Danny muttered as he rubbed his wrists and struggled to open the water.

Khalid shrugged. 'We need to keep you alive if you are to be worth anything.'

Thirsty as he was, Danny paused with the bottle an inch from his lips. 'Worth anything?' he repeated, staring at Khalid in horror.

'Of course!' smiled Rissouli's most dangerous son, bending to pat Danny's cheek. 'Everything, but *everything*, has its value!' He winked, his eyelashes fluttering slowly together in a manner that sent an icy chill shivering up Danny's spine. Rising, he turned and left Danny alone, chuckling as he slammed the tailgate behind him.

Gulping down the water and bread, Danny wondered what on earth Khalid had meant. His whole manner was disturbing, evil even. He was more than just an unscrupulous criminal trying to make a fast buck; something in the depths of those dark eyes spoke of a sadistic cruelty. Khalid, thought Danny, was a man it was best to be as far away from as was humanly possible. Several thousand miles would be about right. Lying in cool, dew-soaked grass on a Perthshire hillside would be just perfect...

Suddenly, there was a thumping on the side of the truck, an unwelcome reminder of where he was. 'Move! Time for your toilet. Be quick or you will have to do it in there!'

Danny shuffled forward, his legs still bound together. They never cut the zip-ties at his ankles. It seemed that even out here in the wilderness they did not want to risk any chance of him escaping. Struggling to his feet he hopped forward in short, unsteady jumps. Nearing the door he lost his balance and put his hand out to steady himself.

'Ow!' He had scraped his palm on a rusty screw sticking out

from one of the repairs to the tailgate. Lifting his hand he saw a spot of blood and an ugly looking tear in the skin. Nothing too serious though, he had done far worse falling off his bike at home.

Sliding to the ground he took the opportunity to have a look at his surroundings. The scenery had changed markedly since the previous day. Trees, shrubs and large-leafed plants grew with robust health from the red soil around them. Above, the sun still shone with aggressive brilliance, but scattered about the sky were puffy white clouds.

They were obviously no longer in the Sahara, and Danny wondered whether they had travelled north to the Mediterranean coast or south, crossing the Sahara to reach tropical Africa. The latter seemed more likely, as it just seemed too hot and humid here to be near the shores of the Mediterranean. There were smells and sounds foreign to him, the guttural cries of unfamiliar birds and the screams of monkeys in the distance. The plants were a vivid green here, unlike their more muted European and North African cousins. No, this place seemed different, somehow more vibrant and exotic. Life seemed to seep from the earth here. Compared to the sterile beauty of the desert, this place was a jostling, chaotic carnival of a landscape, suffused with all the aromas, colours, and sounds of the sensory spectrum. At the same time there was an aura of menace. Behind this overt display of vigorous natural splendour lurked an atmosphere of danger and decay. The suggestion of predators unseen hung in the air like a threat. Danny knew that while a long drawn-out demise in the desert might have been a very real possibility, death was every bit as likely where he was now. The only difference was that here it would probably be short, sharp and fanged.

Back in the truck, Danny prepared to have the zip-ties and hood replaced for the next leg of the journey. Sure enough, Khalid pulled his arms behind his back and bound his wrists as usual. However, before the hood was placed over his head, his captor stuck a large piece of tape over his mouth. It was done too quickly for Danny to object and a moment later the hood was pulled over his head and the world turned black once more.

This was a worrying development. Not only did it make it even more difficult to breathe, it suggested some change in their situation. Danny realised that there was only one reason they would tape his mouth: to prevent him making a noise. And there was only one reason they would need him to be silent: because they were entering an area where there were other human beings. They could simply be passing through a more populous area on their way to somewhere else. However, they had apparently avoided all human habitation for several days without difficulty, so why would they drive through it now? The other possibility was that they were nearing their destination. After all, it was quite probable that the smugglers' base would be in a town or city, much like the house in Chefchaouen.

It had become clear that if he could possibly manage it, he must escape as soon as possible. Things were changing fast and the sooner he was out of it the better. A distant, dusty memory popped into Danny's head of a bookshelf in a bedroom in a house in Cumbria. On the shelf was his dad's collection of what his mum called 'man-literature'. There were thrillers with assassins, spies and ex-special forces treasure hunters; workshop manuals for every car he had ever owned (who knows, maybe he had planned to buy another 1988 Ford Escort one of these days); seventeen *Biggles* books, a *James Bond* compendium and, reverentially placed next to a photo of Great Granddad Lansing, around a dozen books about escaping from prisoner of war camps during World War Two. Danny had read most of them (apart from the workshop manuals) over the years and the escape books were some of the best books that he had ever read.

In one of them (he had forgotten which), the author had mentioned that an escaper's best chance of success lay in getting free whilst he was being transported to his prison. During this time it is difficult to keep a constant eye on a prisoner and of course a truck, railway carriage or a line of marching men is much less secure than a locked room in a big building crawling with armed guards. Once the prisoner had arrived at his place of incarceration his chances of escape became much poorer.

Whether this still held true if you were a scruffy, ginger -haired youth kidnapped by smugglers, rather than an immaculately moustachioed RAF officer captured by the Nazis, remained to be seen. It did seem to make sense though. If the Sons of Rissouli got him to their lair and locked him in some cellar, the likelihood of him being able to escape was virtually nil.

On the face of it Danny's position seemed pretty hopeless: he was bound hand and foot, gagged and blindfolded. Starving, hungry and thirstier than he ever imagined it was possible to be, his body ached from his beating and from being bounced up and down in the back of a truck for four days. Like a fool, he had even managed to cut himself stumbling against the truck's tailgate. No, he had definitely been in better shape.

Before he did anything else, Danny knew he had to get the hood off his head. Once he could see he would be in a much better position to work out how he was going to escape. The hood didn't seem to be tied on too tightly, if he could just get it to snag on something he might be able to wriggle out of it. Suddenly he let out a short snorting laugh. The screw on the tailgate! He had cursed his clumsiness earlier, but perhaps now something good could come from his stumble.

It was a struggle to raise himself to his feet in the lurching truck, but eventually he managed it and started to shuffle slowly forwards. He leant against the tailgate, feeling with his head for the repaired section. He thought he knew roughly where it would be but it was a few frustrating minutes before his forehead came into contact with it. Now came the tricky bit. Slowly he began to run his hooded forehead across the repair, searching for the protruding end of the screw, all the time struggling to stay standing as the truck lurched over uneven tracks.

'MMF! Fumfing, gunmpf!' Danny's curses were muffled by the tape over his mouth, but swearing still had that desired cathartic effect. Yes, he had found the screw all right, the damn thing had taken a chunk out of his forehead. However, it had also torn a hole in the hood, getting hooked up in the fabric. Danny slowly backed away and, as he did, he could feel the hood start to slide from over his head. It was working! He eased the hood past his chin and then, with a bit of a struggle, over his nose. Abruptly, it swept off his head altogether and Danny could see again.

He was still bound and gagged and locked in the back of a truck, but Danny felt like he had fought half the battle - and won! He searched the back of the truck for something he could use to cut the zip-ties on his wrists. Soon he was back on the floor, shuffling along the uneven steel floor like a seal on his belly.

Danny was looking for a sharp piece of metal to cut his bonds and it wasn't long before he found one. A piece of sheet steel had been welded roughly into place not far from the rear of the truck. One of the corners had lifted, caught and been bent out of shape by crates being repeatedly dragged over it.

Turning round, Danny sat so the lip of sharp metal was within reach of his wrists and then started to saw the zip-tie against it. In just a few seconds it snapped and his hands were free. Ripping the tape from his mouth he started to work on freeing his ankles. Again it took just a few seconds to cut the plastic zip-ties. Looking around, he realised he was by no means 'home free'. The truck might be old and rough but it was still robust. The floor was quite clearly too tough to break through and the wooden sides might have been prised apart with a crow-bar or broken with an axe, but Danny had neither at his disposal. He approached the tailgate for a closer look. It comprised two doors that opened outwards, hinged at the sides. They were made of heavy planks of wood set in an iron frame, and secured on the outside by some sort of bolt. Peering through the gap between the doors Danny could just make out a heavy padlock swinging in the sun.

After the elation of escaping from his bonds and hood, his heart now sank in despair. It appeared his efforts had been in vain. Examining the door minutely, he searched every square centimetre for possible weaknesses, but there were none. He did the same with the floor and walls, but failed to find any suggestion of a way out. Sinking to the floor, he sat with his head in his hands.

'C'mon, think, think! There must be a way out of here!' he told himself. He searched his pockets, but a snotty handkerchief and a few Moroccan coins were unlikely to help him. He counted his money: about enough to buy a cold drink at a roadside stall. Not nearly enough to bribe his way to freedom, he reflected. He thought back to his dad's escape books again. Could he do something with his shoelaces perhaps? He was really clutching at straws now. No, it was looking pretty hopeless all round.

He lay back, closing his eyes to think. It seemed there

was no way out and he would discover what Khalid had meant by 'everything has a value' after all. He had made a good effort, though. Nobody could ever say he had not tried. If nothing else he would enjoy the look on Khalid's face when he opened the back of the truck to find him hoodless and making rude gestures with unbound hands.

The truck made a particularly heavy lurch and the roof rattled. Danny opened his eyes. Gazing at the roof for the first time, he realised he had not considered this as a possible escape route. Cursing his stupidity, he jumped up for a closer look and in the gloom he noticed a vent not far from the tailgate. It was a grill of bars, covered on the outside by a flat metal plate, presumably to stop the rain from coming in. The bars were only a few centimetres apart, enough to let air circulate, but clearly nowhere near big enough to let him crawl through. However, the grill appeared to be a single unit which had been screwed into place. If he could remove the whole unit....

He could not reach it from the floor, so he climbed up the doors to get a better look. Slipping his fingers behind a piece of iron framework, he got the toe of his left shoe on a lip of wood. Putting as much weight on his foot as possible he heaved himself upwards. Even though it was difficult to hold on with the truck bouncing and rolling, he could now just about reach the grill and quickly stretched out for the bars. Gripping them with both hands, he swung his feet free.

From this position he could now see that the grill was held in place with four screws. The slot in each screw's head looked like it might just fit the edge of the smallest of the coins in

Danny's pocket. His problem was that he would never be able to hold himself up with one hand, while taking out the screws with his other. He needed some way of holding his weight, but how? He could only balance on the lip of wood for a few seconds.

Dropping back to the floor he chewed his bottom lip thoughtfully for a moment before hitting on a plan. Crouching with a satisfied smile playing on his lips, he pulled the laces from his trainers. They were thick nylon ones that looked like they might just be strong enough for his purpose. Quickly, he tied the ends together with a 'figure of eight' knot that Angus had shown him when they had had gone rock climbing near Dunkeld. He reckoned if it was good enough for rock climbing it should be good enough for this.

He now had a single lace about 250 cm long. At one end he tied a loop big enough to slip a foot into, like a small stirrup. Climbing back up to the grill, he hung on with one hand and tied the other end of the lace to one of the bars. A 'figure of eight' was too tricky to tie with one hand so he just secured it with a few half-hitches.

He then slipped his right foot into the hanging loop and cautiously put his weight on it. The lace did not break. Standing in the loop, he steadied himself with one hand, grabbed a coin from his pocket and started unscrewing the grill from the roof.

Danny quickly realised this was going to be a laborious job. The first screw was extremely difficult to turn with the edge of the coin and shifted by just a quarter of a turn with each attempt. Each time he tried to turn it further, the truck bumped and his hand slipped. His fingers started to ache and standing in the looped shoelace became very tiring, but he carried on regardless. He knew this was his only hope of escape and he had to try with every ounce of his strength to succeed. Failure did not bear thinking about.

The process seemed to take forever. Danny regularly had to step down and rest for a few minutes to regain his strength. He was also starting to hear new sounds outside the truck. Now and again he caught the rumble of passing traffic, even the fleeting snatch of voices, and wondered if they were closing on their destination. Any moment now they could come to a halt and throw open the back of the truck. The thought spurred him on and he attacked the grill with new energy, desperate to escape while he still had the chance.

One by one the screws fell to the floor and he was just beginning to unscrew the third when, with a sudden tearing groan, the grill finally broke free. The extra weight of his body hanging from the lace was too much for the last screws to hold and it tore from the roof, sending the grill and Danny flying to the floor in a thump that shook the truck. He lay still for several nerve-wracking seconds, wondering if his captors had heard the crash or felt him fall. But the engine note did not change and they barrelled along the same as ever; he might just have got away with it.

With a surge of excitement, Danny climbed back up the tailgate to the hole in the ceiling. He was seconds from escape now and his heart raced as the adrenaline coursed in his veins.

Grabbing the edges of the hole with both hands he heaved his head and shoulders up through the opening.

It was early evening and the soft light of the setting sun bathed the passing trees in a wash of gold. A warm wind rushed through his hair and after being locked up for so long he almost laughed with exhilaration. He dragged himself up through the hole and crouched precariously on his hands and knees on the rolling roof.

'All right,' he said to himself. 'Now all I have to do is get down...'

They were rattling along at about fifty miles an hour, the hard-packed earth whizzing past twelve feet below. Any attempt to jump would result in a sickening bouncing tumble, any number of broken bones and the repeated screaming of 'AAARGH!'. So he lay flat on the roof and waited, hoping that it would only be a matter of time before an opportunity arose to climb down. Perhaps they would stop at a junction or slow for a sharp corner.

After half an hour Danny had second thoughts. Slowing down might mean the thugs were pulling into the side of the road to rest or relieve themselves, at which moment they would inevitably see him clinging on to the roof. To be discovered at this stage would be unbearable so he decided there was nothing else for it. He would have to jump from the truck, no matter what the risk was. Whatever happened would have to be better than being caught, beaten, hooded and bound up again.

At that moment he spotted something. A gleaming ribbon

was twisting its way across the landscape like a vast golden serpent. As the vanishing sun set the horizon alight in a long blaze of red, its fire was reflected in the mirror-like surface of a river a few miles up ahead. The road crossed it in a long, low bridge and that, thought Danny, would be his final chance to escape.

He spent those last few minutes on the approach to the river desperately trying to summon his courage. His heart pounded and his breathing quickened. His mouth became bone dry and his legs shook as the bridge drew rapidly nearer. It all came down to this; all the effort and pain of escaping his bonds and removing the vent would be for nothing if he failed in these final seconds.

Unsteadily, Danny rose off his knees and crouched as he watched the bridge draw closer and closer. He tried to guess how fast they were going and how much of a drop there was between the bridge and the surface of the water. Most of all he wondered how deep the water was. Then, all of a sudden, they were on the bridge and Danny was looking over the edge to the dark waters below. The river was a sickeningly long way down, further than he had thought. And although the truck had slowed slightly he guessed they were still doing around forty miles per hour.

If he thought for too long his courage might fail and they would reach the other bank. Steeling himself, he took a deep breath, stood up and jumped.

In that brief moment before he hit the water everything seemed to go quiet. Danny felt a strange sense of calm as the river rushed up to meet him. It was out of his hands now: nothing he could do would halt his fall and with that knowledge all fear deserted him.

He smacked down into the water with an impact that knocked the wind from him. He had landed well, with his feet first and with his arms thrown around his face for protection, but from that height and at that speed the water felt as hard as concrete. Dazed, he fell fast, the dark murkiness enveloping him like a shroud. When he opened his eyes he could see nothing. Suddenly his feet hit the mud of the riverbed and he realised that had the water been any less deep the contact would have injured him. As it was, the stroking of weeds around his legs threatened to entangle and drown him.

For a few endless seconds he was too stunned to do anything but hang motionless in the darkness as he drifted slowly downstream. With a shake of his head he recovered a little, and forced himself to start the long swim upwards. He had never been very good at holding his breath for long and his lungs were already hurting from the effort. He knew he had fallen deep, because above him there was no sign of the surface, just a gradual lightening of the murk.

After a few rapid strokes he saw a sliver of light from the setting sun dancing in the water and knew he must be nearing the surface. He sped towards it, bursting through a couple of seconds later. He threw his head back and gasped deep breaths of the sweet evening air into his aching lungs.

Looking around frantically he half expected a hail of gunfire to rip up the water around him, but it seemed his escape had gone unnoticed. On the other side of the river the road climbed in a long sweeping curve towards a gap between two hills. Trailing its ever-present tail of swirling dust was the smugglers' truck, disappearing into the gathering gloom of the African night.

Treading water in the slow-moving current, Danny smiled. There had been so many moments in the last few days when he had despaired of surviving the week. He was suddenly intensely proud of himself, and could not wait until he saw his Uncle Angus again, to tell him the story of his escape. Just this once, *he* would be the one with the gripping tale of death-defying adventure! Finding Angus might be difficult, but it would be nothing after having stared death in the face. With long, lazy strokes Danny started to swim ashore.

The cool river water seemed to soothe his bruises and ease his aching muscles and it was only once he reached the bank and staggered wearily from the shallows that it occurred to him he might have been swimming with crocodiles...

CHAPTER SIX

By the time Angus had walked back to the pick-up the storm had already begun to die down. The sun was visible again, shining weakly through the haze of airborne dust, and he could no longer feel the stinging pain of sand scouring his face. After a brief assessment of the Toyota's condition, Angus decided it was roadworthy - or at least roadworthy enough to get him away from the immediate vicinity of the two smugglers, who might, at any moment, recover to cause him problems.

There was extensive damage to the right front wing where the driver's side door was heavily dented and its window shattered. The bonnet was bent upwards in a shallow arch and the tyre at that corner had been shredded. However, the battered old vehicle still looked like it would move, so Angus decided to drive, at least until he was out of sight of the smugglers.

A slow drive to the west took him to a place where he felt it was safe to stop and he jumped out, immediately setting to the job of repairing the pick-up. The damaged wing was removed and discarded; it was barely hanging on and Angus felt it was only a matter of time before it disintegrated, possibly shredding another tyre. He flattened the bonnet by climbing on to it and jumping up and down. It was never going to be in showroom condition again anyway, but at least he could now open and close it without resorting to the use of a hammer and the biggest screwdriver in his tool-kit.

An inspection of the engine revealed that it had miraculously escaped damage. There seemed to be no leakage of oil or diesel and none of the ancillary equipment seemed affected. It started up with no unusual noises, the alternator gave a good current and the radiator did not appear to have been holed. In fact, thought Angus, the old girl seemed to be running sweeter than she had been before. Perhaps he ought to crash his cars into other vehicles more often...

It did not take long to replace the damaged wheel with one of the spares, and he was soon tearing further west across the desert. The sooner he could get onto good roads the better. Here he had an advantage. The smugglers would need to travel by the back roads and through the isolated interior of the Sahara if they were to reach Senegal and Dakar unnoticed. Those routes would be longer and slower than taking the roads Angus (as a law abiding citizen) could travel by. He would take the motorway that ran down the West-African coast.

As soon as he reached the tarmac roads near Zagora he re-inflated his tyres to highway pressures and had another quick look round the vehicle to make sure nothing was going to fall off. Taking full advantage of the smooth surface he gunned the Toyota along as fast as it would go and tried not to think of what might be happening to Danny. As he drove, he dismantled the Brunton automatic he had taken off the smuggler, tossing the parts out of the broken side-window, one piece every few miles. Despite the fact it might prove useful over the next few days, he had no desire to keep it. Not only did he have to pass through Mauritanian and Senegalese customs in the next few days, but handguns had always made him uncomfortable. It gave him the creeps that people could invest so much effort into engineering a tool whose only purpose was to kill human beings.

North of Ouarzazate he turned on to the Agadir road, which wound its way through waterless, monolithic peaks on its journey to the Atlantic. From here, the navigation was simple: follow the road ahead to its junction with the N1. At the junction turn left, stop when you get to Dakar. Of course, there were still 3000 kilometres of African traffic and two border posts to negotiate, but Angus thought he could reach Dakar in about three days without too much difficulty.

The landscape began to flatten out as the N1 took him into the Western Sahara, the parched southern region of Morocco. Angus understood it to be empty save for a few rebellious Bedouin and some famously bad-tempered camels. The region lacked the rugged beauty of the north and consisted of monotonous desert plains that seemed to stretch on into infinity. Ephemeral traces of industry merely emphasised the emptiness. Along the road lay the occasional carcass of a rusting oil drum with ribs of iron pointing skywards like the ragged remains of a rotting corpse. The trucks that travelled this route, transporting cargo of all descriptions between North and Tropical Africa, had left clear markers of their passing: a torn fragment of tyre, an unidentified piece of machinery, a length of rope that had once been used to secure a load. This was country through which one passed. Only the Bedouin were tough enough to live here.

Here and there, thin fingers of sand stretched across the tarmac, as though the desert was trying to claw back this long strand of territory. Along the side of the road ran a line of pylons, the two arteries of communication huddling together as though frightened by the surrounding wilderness. It was as barren a landscape as Angus had ever seen and its monotony did not help his concentration.

He had been awake for a very long time now, since the morning before in fact, and his head and shoulders ached with fatigue. In the west, the sun had begun its slow change to red, signalling the end of another day. He knew he could not fight sleep for much longer, his eyelids seemed to be forcing themselves together with a super-human strength and his chin felt like it was attached to his chest by elastic.

At last he surrendered to exhaustion and pulled off the tarmac, into the desert. The road ran just a few hundred metres from the coast here and Angus parked at the top of the rugged cliffs that marked the boundary between Africa and the Atlantic. The angry sea, raised by a hot trade wind, foamed and spat among the rocks below. Unable to summon up the energy to pitch the tent, Angus fell asleep in the cab, the roar of the surf a lullaby that drowned out his fears for Danny.

★ ★ ★

The next day, having spent the morning negotiating the

chaotic shambles of Mauritanian Customs, Angus continued south towards Senegal. Still the parched landscape bore only infrequent traces of human settlement. There were occasional small, fly-blown villages and from time to time he would see the railway that, like the road, clung nervously to the Atlantic coast. Only once did he see a train rumbling along its tracks. It was the longest he had ever seen, stretching for what seemed like miles. In fact, it was so long he could not see both ends at once and by the time the rear had come within sight the front had disappeared into the distance. It clanked along not much faster than walking speed, making its way north across the desert.

Slowly, almost imperceptibly, the landscape became greener as he travelled south. Instead of the sand and rock that covered the north of the country, dry grass, low scrub and even trees started to appear. The air became noticeably more humid as white clouds decorated the deep blue sky. This new humidity was sticky and uncomfortable, but at least the choking dust, which had blown in through the broken window during his drive through the waterless desert, was no longer a problem. Even the earth itself began to change colour. Iron in the soil had turned it from a soft golden brown to a burnt red, the colour of terracotta flower pots.

As Angus neared the grubby border town of Rosso on the Senegal River the following morning, heavy grey clouds, pregnant with the promise of rain, lay in a grey blanket across the expectant landscape. It was the end of the dry season and the rains that would bring an explosion of growth to the umber soil were only hours away.

The people he passed on the road shot frequent glances skyward as they walked. The children seemed strangely excited, playing more aggressively and laughing more loudly than normal. Goats and donkeys were already huddled beneath trees, claiming their spot under the flimsy shelter of the overhanging branches. The whole country seemed to be on tenterhooks, waiting for the inevitable downpour. Of course, the rain had a very different significance here. Back home it meant being cold and wet, or trapped indoors until you were bored rigid. Here it was the very source of life. Without it, the earth would simply dry up and blow away on the wind.

Angus crossed the Senegal River in the early afternoon on a ferry crammed with cars and mopeds, donkeys and goats, chickens, children and boxes of fruit. More than one passenger shook him by the hand, in the gentle West-African manner, and welcomed him to Senegal. Angus wished he was only travelling to see the world, wished he didn't have a nephew to rescue and gun-runners to overcome. Staring a little sadly at the clamouring assembly of humanity ranged about him, he thought how wonderful it would be to simply disappear into the heart of the Sahel for a while and learn more about these people and their lives on the southern fringes of the Sahara. He allowed himself to daydream, to picture himself travelling by the least known roads and visiting the most remote communities. He knew he would be able to lose himself for weeks, absorbing the culture, meeting new friends, experiencing life the way the locals lived it.

With a metallic groan the ferry shuddered along its length, bringing Angus back from his reverie with a bump. They had reached the other side of the river and with it, Senegal. As he sat at the steering wheel, waiting to disembark, Angus considered his next move. It wasn't far to Dakar now: he should reach it the following day with ease. What he really needed was a place to stop and think, a place where he could calmly formulate a rescue plan. He could really do with a proper feed and a good bed for the night as well. Driving all day and sleeping in the car was starting to take its toll. Looking at the map he decided to head for Saint-Louis, about seventy miles to the south.

★ ★ ★

Saint-Louis was a hub for travellers passing between Tropical and Saharan Africa, and from what Angus could gather it had been so for centuries. It was a picturesque town, slowly crumbling into a lagoon on the Atlantic coast.

Not long after he had checked into a hotel on Saint-Louis's main island, the downpour began. Angus's room had a balcony overhanging the water where he sat and rested for a while, just listening to the rain hammering a tattoo on the tin roof. It hissed across the lagoon in great waves and ran in torrents from the roofs and gutters of the surrounding buildings, splashing noisily to the ground in ever-expanding puddles. One of the brightly painted local fishing boats – a pirogue, he remembered – chugged slowly by with a load of fish for the market. A boy of about seven, feet wide apart and toes curled over the gunwales, stood astride its bows, arms in the air and laughing at the sky.

Angus shook his head and sighed. Oh, to be so carefree!

Bending to rummage in a holdall, he pulled out a street-map of Dakar and a short stub of pencil. He spread out the map on the rickety iron table and gazed distractedly at the mass of streets. In all his adventures, in all the dumb scrapes and silly situations he had got himself into, it had never gone as badly as this. Nothing he had ever done had had the same potential for such tragic consequences. Of course, up till now he had only had himself to worry about. Now that he had his nephew to look after, he knew he really should not go about behaving as though nothing had changed. He cursed himself under his breath with the rudest insult he could think of – it was Spanish and involved goats. It made him feel no better.

At that moment, there was a knock at the door and into his room padded an old lady wrapped in a colourful dress and capped with a thick knot of tightly curled grey hair. She placed an enormous plate of Senegalese tieboudeinne on his table along with a cold drink. Angus's eyes were already eating up the vision of the fish, vegetables and rice cooked in tomato juice when, with the gently sympathetic smile of a woman who has been a mother to many, she said: 'You are tired. You look older than your years.'

Angus wondered vaguely how she knew how old he was. 'Yes. I've had a hard few days.'

'Well, tonight you will sleep very soundly. We have soft

beds here and the noise of the rain…' She stopped and looked searchingly into his grey eyes. Seeming to find what she was looking for, she straightened, clapped her hands and said, 'Do not worry, child. I'm sure you will find what you are looking for. Here… eat. My tieboudeinne is the best in Senegal!' She smiled again, then turned and shuffled softly from the room.

Angus watched the lady leave with mixed feelings. It had been a long time since anyone had called him 'child', and in other circumstances he might have found it irritating. However, her motherly interruption had been a welcome reminder of humanity. She had succeeded where the Spanish insult had failed. She had made him feel slightly better.

Angus took an experimental mouthful of the tieboudeinne. He had to admit, it was extremely good. Suddenly he realised how ravenous he was. He hadn't eaten properly for days, simply cramming a muesli bar down his gullet whenever he remembered. As he hoovered up the huge plateful he felt supremely grateful to the old lady. Her meal was completing the job her kind words had begun.

Throwing his fork down on the empty plate with satisfaction, he regarded the map of Dakar with new resolve. The city was sprawled untidily across a ragged, hook-shaped peninsula which jutted out into the Atlantic. In the east of the city lay the rough dockyard area. He expected it to be a complicated warren of warehouses, workshops and offices. It was here that the Sons of Rissouli had their premises. In the west of the city - hidden amongst what looked, from the more spacious feel of the map, to be the houses of Senegal's most affluent residents - was their headquarters.

Angus wondered if he should contact the British Embassy or the Senegalese Police as soon as he arrived in Dakar, but then decided against it. Unfortunately, he only had the word of a frightened smuggler to suggest Danny was in Senegal at all. Neither authority would be likely to investigate further on the say-so of freelance journalist. Particularly one who had gathered his information by sticking a gun in the belly of a criminal.

It seemed that the best option would be to take a look at the addresses he had been given. If he could find some proof that Danny was being held prisoner there, or indeed that any illegal activity was taking place, he might be able to persuade the authorities to act. Of course the best way to 'take a look' would be to break in and have a poke around. Not for the first time, Angus realised how lucky he was that, of all his less respectable talents, breaking-and-entering seemed to be the one that came most naturally. There must have been a cat-burglar somewhere in the McKinlay family history.

He figured the Sons of Rissouli would be most likely to hold Danny in the windowless seclusion of the warehouse with its quiet, industrialised surroundings. A residential house, with all its windows, doors and nosy neighbours, would make a much less secure prison. He would have a look at the warehouse first and, if he found nothing, move onto the gang's headquarters on the Route de la Corniche-Ouest.

Fortunately, in the Toyota's toolkit (hidden under

a particularly filthy selection of rags, old oil filters, rusty nuts and bolts and some broken hacksaw blades) was what Angus called his 'Raffles' kit. He had named it after the original 'gentleman thief' whose adventures Angus had read as a boy. It had taken him years to acquire its contents, often from rather unsavoury sources, but it had got him into more places than he cared to remember – or would ever admit. The more he thought about the possibilities of Danny's imprisonment, the more he thanked his lucky stars he had brought the kit with him.

It comprised a green canvas shoulder bag stuffed with everything a burglar would need. Not only did it contain basic tools like pliers and glass cutters, it also included some more specialist items: a nine-piece lock pick set, a selection of bump keys, a stethoscope, a slim jim tool for breaking into cars and, scrawled in the spidery hand of a man he had met in Hong Kong, a list of factory-set combinations for the world's five largest safe manufacturers.

Scrutinising the map, he found the street where the warehouse was located and circled it with his pencil. Tomorrow, he decided, he would drive the last one hundred and sixty miles to Dakar, find a quiet spot and wait for darkness to fall. Realising there wasn't much more he could do in the way of preparation, Angus tucked the map back into the holdall and stood up. Stretching, he yawned and thought about brushing his teeth.

'Sod it!' he said to the rain-filled world outside his balcony. Stumbling the six short steps to his bed, he barely paused to remove his trousers and shirt before collapsing gratefully onto the sheets. It was just as the old lady had promised; the bed was soft and the hissing of rain on the tin roof sent him quickly into the deepest of sleeps.

★ ★ ★

Late the following night, Angus emerged silently from the alley with the 'Raffles' kit tucked under his arm. He had parked in the outskirts of the Dakar docks, not far from the warehouse. This part of town was very run-down and poorly lit. The moon and stars had been blotted out by the thick cloud-cover, and only a few flickering street lamps threw their feeble orange glow into the darkness. But that suited Angus just fine. As far as he was concerned the darker it was, the better.

Angus had been itching to get a look at the warehouse since arriving at lunchtime. However, he knew that as a white guy in a pink pick-up truck, he stood out like a sore thumb. So he had waited impatiently in the alley, wondering where Danny was and what might be happening to him, fervently hoping he was not too late. He had to find his nephew alive and well. He *needed* to.

The activity of the day had continued for several hours after sunset. Only after midnight had silence finally fallen, allowing Angus to feel it was safe to get out and look around.

Passing stealthily from one inky black shadow to the next, he stopped every few paces to listen. The silence thundered in his ears: it was almost *too* quiet. Although, in his experience, silence had always been a good sign. It meant he was alone. It was when the shouting and loud noises started that you had to worry.

He tip-toed onwards, to the warehouse, splashing through unseen puddles, until he arrived, with a pounding heart, at the entrance.

First things first, he thought. He must do a circular reconnaissance of the whole warehouse, to see what buildings surrounded it and search for weaknesses in the outer ring of security. Smiling to himself in the darkness, he remembered the time he had spent an hour picking the lock of an office in Bucharest. When he had finally succeeded in opening the door he had discovered that a window facing on to a quiet alley at the back had been left wide open.

An air of decay and defeat hung over this peripheral corner of the city's docklands. Poverty was etched into the very fabric of the near-derelict buildings; all had been repeatedly repaired with scrap timber, broken pallets, and even old road signs. Many of the small paned windows were broken, or had been replaced with clear polythene.

By contrast, the Sons of Rissouli had the largest and newest building in the area, a bold new construction of top quality galvanised steel. Protected by a high chain link fence, and with its own lighting at the entrance, it looked entirely out of place among the rusting, rotting workshops that surrounded it. Either the Sons of Rissouli were spearheading urban regeneration, or they had a more disreputable reason for tucking themselves away from the heart of the docks and, crucially, from the noses of curious customs officials. Angus had little doubt which was the most likely explanation.

The front gate was too brightly lit for a surreptitious entrance, so Angus decided to take a look at the back of the building, where sections of the perimeter fence were cloaked in shadow. From a distance, he chose his spot carefully and hurried towards the darkest shadow, where he was hidden from general view by a pile of old crates. Even in daylight, any passersby would be unlikely to spot him, but in the darkness he would be well-nigh invisible.

After a quick check around to confirm he was alone, Angus approached the fence. It looked like a fairly standard chain link, roughly ten feet high and held up with iron posts set in concrete. In normal circumstances he would have been over it in seconds, but in this case the vicious-looking coils of razor wire at the top made him think twice.

The good news was that it appeared to have no alarm. A fibre optic cable or taught-wire system would be easy to spot. There might be a vibration sensor attached to the fence, but Angus doubted it.

Crouching down, he examined the ground at the foot of the fence for signs of passive magnetic detection, or some similar buried alarm system. If one had been installed, there would be long sections of new concrete amongst the old stuff. At his feet was a patchwork of old concrete and tarmac, with only the bases of the fence posts looking new. It seemed like getting past the fence, at least, should not present too many difficulties.

He had two options: grab a tarpaulin from the back of the Toyota and drape it over the razor-wire to let him climb over; or cut a hole in the fence with his wire cutters. He went with the latter. Scrabbling over loosely coiled razor-wire ten feet above the ground would be noisy, could attract the attention of anyone who might happen along and would ruin a perfectly good tarpaulin. He could quite easily make a small hole in the fence; the wire-cutters were extremely sharp and had been designed to hold both ends of the wire after it had been cut. They could be released quietly, without a loud 'TWANG!' and a rattle of the fence. It also meant that if vibration sensors *had* been fitted, he was less likely to set them off.

Angus held his breath as he cut and released the first wire. It separated without an accompaniment of bells or flashing lights. He breathed once more and a few minutes later had cut a hole like a large cat-flap in the fence, close to the ground. Easing the flap up carefully, he wriggled through, taking care not to touch the sides. Once on the other side, he pulled one of the crates over so it covered the hole, pushed the wire back into place and secured his 'cat-flap' with a few twists of copper wire from his kit. The hole was invisible to anything but the closest inspection.

Putting his cutters away, he now pulled out an electronic device that looked a bit like a small video camera. In fact it was a night vision scope. Small, light and relatively cheap, Angus had bought it online only a few months before. Flicking it on, he peered through it at the dark bulk of the warehouse about twenty metres away.

'Heh, heh!' he chuckled softly. 'Gotta love the internet!'

To the naked eye the rear of the warehouse was a black silhouette. Through the scope, it was an entirely different picture. He could see the whole scene in livid green detail, from the black puddles stretched across the uneven concrete at his feet to the eaves of the warehouse roof. It was as though the whole area was bathed in a soft emerald twilight.

Two things immediately caught his attention. The first was a door in the warehouse wall. It had no glass or other obvious weakness and was secured with a heavy padlock. Nevertheless, it might provide a way in. The second was a large security lamp, the kind that uses an infra-red sensor to detect minute changes in temperature, fixed to the wall directly above the door. He would have to be careful not to trigger it.

Further inspection revealed something else. On the left of the building, tucked almost out of sight under the guttering, was a tiny grey box. Increasing the magnification of the scope, its purpose became evident: it was a CCTV camera. At best, the back of the warehouse was being recorded. At worst, it was being monitored by a security guard at that very moment.

Realising that he might already have been spotted, Angus held his breath as a tingle of apprehension shivered between his shoulder blades. He became very aware of the silence again, his ears straining for evidence that a pursuit had begun. But nothing disturbed the hot night air. Looking around, he saw he was still cloaked in shadow, as was most of the area behind the warehouse. The chances of anyone having seen him were pretty slim. He relaxed again – just a little – and thought about his next move.

While he was relatively safe where he was, Angus was well aware that if he triggered the infra-red security light, he would be lit up like a Christmas tree and would probably have the Sons of Rissouli down on him in an instant. Being shot at was becoming tiresome, so he decided to do all he could to avoid it. The novelty had most definitely worn off.

Fortunately, he knew a few things about these passive infra-red security lights and was fairly confident he could get to the door without setting it off. Angus didn't know exactly how hot this steaming African night was, but it had to be above 30 degrees Celsius. With the average body temperature of a person being 37, it might just mean the light's sensor would be slow to register him, the difference in temperature being too small. Most of these infra-red security lights had a range of about twelve to fifteen metres; as long as he stayed further than that distance from the lamp he ought to be able to reach the building without setting it off. It would mean crossing over to the warehouse at its far corner, but this would present no problems.

He also knew that the lights usually had an arc of detection which spanned around 120 degrees, and, conveniently, that there was usually a 'blind-spot' directly under the lamp, just where the door was located.

Angus moved off down the fence, staying close to it and as far as he could get from the security light. He crossed the open ground and reached the corner of the warehouse without difficulty. Now came the tricky bit. He started to edge his way along the wall, slowly at first, but soon gaining confidence. Shortly, he was standing directly below the security light in the shallow doorway. He kept himself pressed close against the door though as the security light's 'blind spot' would only be about 30 centimetres deep.

Pulling the 'Raffles' kit from under his armpit, he unzipped it and extracted a small bunch of bump keys that would enable him to opens all locks of a particular type. He had bump keys for about twenty different manufacturers and models of lock. He hoped luck would be on his side and one of them would fit, because picking a lock the traditional way was a long and tiresome business at the best of times; trying to do it in the dark while pressed flat against the door would be well-nigh impossible.

After a few failed attempts, he at last found one that slotted in perfectly. There was a brief rattle and clunk as he drove the key home, and then the padlock popped open, echoing conspicuously into the night. It sounded uncomfortably loud in the surrounding silence and Angus's heart pounded a little harder. He still did not know if the Sons of Rissouli had security guards on site. He could be about to walk into a very nasty situation and announcing his arrival with excessive noise would be unlikely to improve things.

Sliding the bolt back, he eased the door open a few inches and peered inside. As he had expected, it was pitch black, so he pulled out the night vision scope to get a better look. In the green light he could see rows and rows of high shelves packed with crates of all sizes. Disappointingly, but not surprisingly, there was no sign of Danny. It would have been nice to have found his nephew unharmed, unguarded and ready to be rescued, but that would have been asking too much. Experience had taught him that things didn't usually fall into place so easily.

At the far end of the warehouse was a small office sectioned off from the rest of the building by fibreboard walls. It had a small window, through which no light shone. Angus guessed that if there were any guards on site, they would spend most of their time here, whereas the complete, undisturbed darkness indicated he was alone. He stepped inside and closed the door behind him.

It seemed even quieter in the dark interior of the warehouse than it had been outside. No movement stirred the stagnant air, not the slightest rustle of sound or glimmer of light disturbed the crypt-like gloom. Using the scope, Angus searched the walls and ceiling for signs of a burglar alarm. He could see nothing. It seemed the Sons of Rissouli were confident that the razor wire, camera and security lights were enough to keep intruders at bay.

He turned the night vision scope off and put it away. He could use a normal torch as there was no-one around to see its light. Flicking it on, he started to pad slowly up and down the aisles between the shelving, sweeping the beam ahead of him.

There were hundreds of stacked crates, of all shapes and sizes, and although some were made of wooden planking and others of steel they all had two things in common: they were all painted the same shade of olive green and all had an identical sticky label pasted to one end - a white square bearing the Brunton Armaments logo at the top. Below was a list of contents, a date of packing, a shipment number and an 'End User Certificate' number. This, Angus knew, was a written promise from the government to an arms supplier that the hardware would not be sold on to another group; like terrorists, or governments on the UN's banned list. He noticed there were no crates with the names of other arms manufacturers on them. Something about the Brunton hardware made it either particularly attractive or particularly easy to get hold of. One thing was certain though; there was a huge range of equipment here: handguns, machine guns, grenades – even rocket launchers.

As he approached the little fibreboard office, he noticed a large table strewn with metal parts and polythene. Next to the table were a number of steel drums, similar to oil drums. There were also about two dozen white plastic sacks, bulging with some granular material. Both the steel drums and the sacks were emblazoned with the words: 'Senegal Chemical Company – Agricultural Fertiliser'.

Closer inspection of the metal parts on the table revealed they were pieces of a rocket launcher. Like the handguns found by the police in London, the serial numbers had been ground off. One part, the weapon's trigger mechanism, had been carefully wrapped in polythene.

So, it appeared that The Sons of Rissouli were concealing

arms in barrels full of fertiliser in order to smuggle them out of Senegal. But how were the Sons of Rissouli getting hold of the guns in the first place? Were they were stealing them from the Senegalese Army? Or was a corrupt Senegalese official providing the smugglers with End User Certificates so they could buy the guns straight from Brunton Armaments? If that was the case they must either have lied convincingly enough to make Brunton believe they were legitimate, or Brunton was somehow complicit in the scam.

Angus paused suddenly and smiled as something occurred to him. He retraced his steps to the shelves sweeping his torch across the crates until he found what he was looking for: an unopened one. It was on a low shelf. He stooped to read its label: 'Brunton Armaments – 9mm Automatic', the same type of weapon that the British Police had taken from the drug-dealers in London.

He pulled the crate onto the floor and examined the two hard plastic straps that held it closed. They were secured with a tin seal marked with the Brunton Armaments logo and a serial number. No, these crates had definitely not been opened since they had left the factory.

Using his penknife, he cut the plastic straps and then prised open the lid. Inside were half a dozen handguns, each carefully wrapped in brown paper. He pulled one of the weapons out and tore off its wrapping, examining the area next to the trigger guard. Where there should have been a serial number there was only a small, polished rectangle.

Angus laughed quietly. 'You bloody fools! I have you

banged to rights!' His voice echoed eerily in the darkness, like a snigger at a funeral.

To prevent the weapons from being traced to a particular shipment or country, the serial numbers had been ground off. Not trusting the Sons of Rissouli to do the job properly, somebody at the Brunton factory had done it. Fortunately, their mistrust had given Angus the evidence he needed to implicate them - no honest arms manufacturer would grind the serial numbers from their own products.

He crossed to the office, trying the door and finding it unlocked. Inside was a desk with a lamp, a computer and a fan. Against one wall stood a filing cabinet and on the floor lay a threadbare rug. There was a leather chair behind the desk and another, less comfortable looking one, under the window. On the wall beside the desk was a mirror. Angus smiled at this peculiar evidence of vanity in such a utilitarian space.

Sweeping the beam of his torch down the filing cabinet he read the little yellow labels on the front of each drawer, looking for something that might be incriminating. Pulling open the drawer marked 'Shipping Labels', he thumbed through the cardboard document pockets inside. The pockets were labelled alphabetically and only a few contained labels, but the addresses on them made very interesting reading. There were two addresses in Europe; one in Algericas in Spain, the second an address in Marseille. Of course, once military hardware had been smuggled into France or Spain, it could be transported throughout the European Community without difficulty. This, he reasoned, was presumably how the 9mm automatics had turned up in London.

The labels did not just show destinations in Europe, however, they had also been printed with addresses in the USA, South Africa and the Republic of Sudan. Angus felt anger rising in his chest as he thought about the pain and suffering the greed of Brunton Armaments and the Sons of Rissouli must have caused. He thought about people striving to survive in ghettos, townships and refugee camps. He thought about a man found floating face down in the Thames and a boy called Gareth Desray, whose brain had decorated an alley in East London. All to pay for shiny black four-wheel drives, a villa on the West African coast and who knows what luxuries for Brunton Armaments' board of directors.

Flicking open the last pocket in the drawer, Angus peered at the address on a thick wodge of labels held together with an elastic band. There were at least a hundred in the bundle, signifying an important destination for the smuggled arms. Reading the bold black lettering in the yellow light of his torch, a tingle crept slowly up the back of his scalp as he realised the significance of what he was looking at.

The address was that of an agricultural wholesaler in Peshawar, Pakistan. Angus knew that Pakistan was an 'approved' government that would have no difficulty getting weapons for its army through ordinary, legitimate channels. He also knew that Peshawar was right on the border with Afghanistan, the home of the Taliban, the home of Al Qaeda!

Suddenly this smuggling operation took on a whole new colour. These weapons were not just getting into the hands of common or garden thugs and drug-dealers, they were heading for the eager hands of international terrorists. These machine guns, grenades and rocket launchers were heading for a place where they would be used against UN peacekeepers, whose helicopters might very well be blown out of the sky by a terrorist wielding a British-made rocket launcher. Was Lord Thomas Brunton himself involved in a scheme that was endangering the lives of servicemen from his own country?

Angus was so wrapped up in his thoughts that the first he knew of the gun pointing directly at the back of his head was the smooth, metallic click as its slide was eased back. He didn't wait to find out if he was about be shot or held hostage. Diving for the desk, he snatched up the first thing his hand fell upon, the fan. He hurled it straight behind him in the desperate hope it might knock the gun from the hand that held it. At the same moment a blinding flash and thunderous detonation rattled the flimsy walls of the office.

Something hit Angus on the side of the head and he fell backwards. An explosion of pain surged through his skull and he could see nothing but dancing lights. In his ears a high pitched ringing threatened to deafen him until, slowly, a wave of nausea rose from his gut and engulfed him. Finally giving up the struggle, he slipped helplessly into unconsciousness.

★ ★ ★

He wasn't sure exactly how long he had been unconscious. Long enough for the Sons of Rissouli to tie him to a chair and wrap a bandage round his head, that much was clear. Although, 'bandage' was being over-generous; it was more a filthy rag. They had obviously not been in too much of a rush to apply it either, as his shirt was almost completely red from the blood that had flowed from his wound. He felt desperately weak and his head throbbed with waves of pain.

A man appeared slowly through the mists of Angus's insensibility. Angus recognised him: he had been at the well in Algeria. In a black shirt and trousers, he stood a few paces away, up-lit by the glow of the desk lamp. A sinister figure, his aquiline features were thrown into sharp relief by the orange light. Above him, his shadow clung to the ceiling like an angel of death. The thug's face cracked into a grin, throwing dark lines of shadow across his cheekbones.

'You are a lucky man.'

'Well, I guess that depends on your definition of lucky...' Angus licked his lips. He could taste the dried blood crusting on his face.

'You have done some stupid things. When you broke into my warehouse, you missed the motion-sensor…' Noticing Angus's expression, he explained, 'Oh, you should watch where you're going. You see, it's at floor level. You tripped it as soon as you set foot inside.' His lips parted in a self-satisfied smile. 'Then you threw a fan at me. Normally that would be reason enough for me to kill you. I am also quite sure you are the fool who killed two of my men in the desert. You are *very* lucky to be alive. I rarely miss my target. In fact…' a curl of amusement flickered on the gangster's lips, '…I think this might be the first time!'

'It doesn't feel like you missed!'

'Ha!' The comment was dismissed with a wave. 'You are still alive. If I had hit my target, my men would be scraping your brains off the walls.'

'So why am I alive now?'

'Because I am curious. I want to know who you are. I want to know why you are so interested in my business. Of course, you *will* die, but only once you have told me what you are up to. Please do not make me torture you. More than is necessary, that is.'

Angus could tell he was not kidding. In fact, he got the impression that any resistance would be relished by the thug as an excuse for violence.

Suddenly, the thug's relaxed posture changed. He straightened, the muscles in his cheeks tensed and his eyes narrowed with suspicion: 'You are British. Are you working for Thomas Brunton? Is he planning to double-cross me?'

So Thomas Brunton *was* involved! Angus had suspected as much, but now he knew; the thug had mentioned him by name.

'Hey! I asked you a question! You want to play games with me?'

A dark blur flashed in from Angus's left and a stinging pain burst in his ear. His head snapped round and his vision swam briefly. It took him a second or two to realise he'd been punched. He shook his head in an effort to clear the fog that seemed to have descended upon his mind. He must stay sharp. He must stay focused. It was the only way to find out what was going on here. It was the only way to find out what had happened to Danny… it was the only way to stay alive.

The journalist in him was desperate to know how the Sons of Rissouli were getting hold of Brunton weapons and if Lord Thomas Brunton was personally involved. But Danny was more important. He simply *had* to know what had happened to his nephew.

The thug was shouting now. 'Why were you spying on us in the desert? Why did you follow us here? Who are you?' He drew closer, seething hatred and deep suspicion in his eyes. He took a deep breath, as though struggling to control a savage anger. 'Are you working for Brunton?!' he yelled, fists clenched tightly by his side, ready to be swung. Angus realised there must be no trust at all between Brunton and the Sons of Rissouli. They worked together out of necessity, not because they had warm and fuzzy feelings for each other. He decided he must exploit this lack of trust - use it to find out what he needed to know.

'Perhaps. Tell me what you did with my nephew and I will tell you all you want to know.'

A shadow of doubt passed across the thug's face. 'Your nephew is dead. He tried to escape, so we killed him!'

Angus stared. Slowly, through the dark stain of dried blood that covered his face, a wide, white-toothed smile broke. 'HA-ha! The kid escaped!' He laughed, a little hysterically, a broken cackle in the angry silence. 'Sorry, but I have met too many liars to be fooled by you!'

'WE KILLED HIM!' shouted the thug. He lunged forwards and wrapped his hands around Angus's throat, trying to strangle him into silence. But there was no conviction in his voice and his eyes failed to meet Angus's; Danny had escaped and they both knew it. As Angus's laugh turned to a gasping choke, the thug stepped back and threw another vicious punch.

For the already weakened Angus, it was a hammer blow. His vision darkened and he was aware that his head was rolling loosely between his shoulders. As he began to fall back into unconsciousness, he could hear the gangster's voice, faint and distant through the fug…

'Ahh! … Stay awake you pig! What were you doing for Brunton? What was the plan…?'

Another blow smashed into his left ear, then another; but Angus was too far gone to react, even if he could still hear.

'Stay awake!' A pause. Then, close by, the words whispered in his ear, 'I will be back tomorrow night, pig. You cannot stay asleep forever. Until then, my men will make sure that *you* do not escape.'

CHAPTER SEVEN

Grabbing handfuls of grass and mud, Danny pulled himself wearily up the river-bank. Reaching the top he saw that the sun was just disappearing behind the western horizon. As it went, it sent skywards a single ray of ashen light, the final throes of a dying day. Heavy, ominous clouds were rolling in from the south, reducing the world to a narrow fissure between earth and sky.

He could smell the rain coming, the sweet, heady scent of an impending deluge. As he threw back his head to examine the black clouds blotting out the evening sky, he heard the first crack of thunder. It made him wonder where Angus was at that moment. Perhaps somewhere nearby, also watching the sky and waiting for the rain? It was unlikely, though. It was more probable that he was still in Algeria, searching for him amongst the dunes.

A wayward thought caught him unprepared: what if Angus was dead? What if the Sons of Rissouli had caught him and murdered him? Perhaps his corpse was, at this very moment, lying in the sand under the Saharan stars. With a shudder, he dismissed the thought. His uncle had proven many times before that he was bullet-proof. Hopefully he remained so.

Danny looked up and down the road, unsure for a moment which way to go. In the direction he had come from lay wild, unpopulated country; there seemed little point in going that way. But the other direction was the one in which the Sons of Rissouli thugs were travelling and they might discover his escape at any moment, returning along the road to look for him. In the end, he decided to follow his captors west, despite the risks.

It seemed likely that Khalid was heading for his headquarters, which were most likely to be in a town, like the house in Chefchaouen. Where there was a town, there would be people who could help him. So, turning west, he began his long walk into the night.

It was not long before the rain started. Danny heard it approaching, hissing through the trees in a downpour, bouncing and clattering off the leaves and turning the cracked earth to mud. It arrived all of a sudden, in a grey curtain, the heaviest rain Danny had ever experienced; a breathtaking torrent of water that soaked him to the skin in seconds.

'I was drier in the flipping river!' he grumbled, hunching his shoulders and wondering if his luck would ever change. He trudged slowly along the muddy road, almost blind in the pitch darkness, for nearly three hours before he gave up. The adrenalin that had got him through the escape had finally run out. He was cold, soaking wet and completely exhausted. Feeling his way through the thick undergrowth, he made his way towards the looming black bulk of a tree that stood close by the roadside. Sitting down in the shelter of its branches, he wrapped his arms around himself in a futile effort to stay warm. Within moments he was fast asleep.

★ ★ ★

He woke with a start. Peering anxiously into the darkness of the forest he wondered if some sixth sense - some animal instinct for danger - had roused him from his sleep. But no, a gurgling growl from his guts told him he had been roused by a more mundane sense: hunger. Danny paused in his train of thought. Was hunger a sense? he wondered. He felt it ought to be. He counted them off on his fingers: 'Okay. One… sight. Two… hearing. Three… touch. Four… smell. Five… oh… taste. Of course.' But wasn't hunger connected to taste and smell? Anyone who had passed a chip shop around dinner-time could testify to that.

He could feel his heart beating, thumping against his ribs. Was that normal? Perhaps it was just because it was so quiet. He strained his ears to catch the slightest sound from the surrounding jungle, but could hear nothing above the pounding in his chest. His stomach growled again.

'This is ridiculous!' he said out loud. The hunger, exhaustion and the constant battle against fear were taking their toll. His mind was wandering and his resolve weakening; he needed to take action, to do something positive to improve his situation. And he needed to do it now.

He rubbed his eyes, dragged himself to his feet and, as he made his way back to the road, realised the rain had stopped, leaving long puddles that pockmarked the uneven roadway. The silvery light of the moon and stars shone through the fragments of heavy cloud scattered across the sky.

Walking made him feel a little better and he almost started to feel optimistic. He reminded himself that he had escaped from the bad guys, after all. Okay, so he was tired and he was hungry, but these were fairly minor complaints compared to being bound and gagged and in the hands of murderous criminals.

He had not been walking long when the unmistakeable rumbling of a diesel truck engine behind him made him turn and, almost instinctively, dive behind a bush. After a moment's panic, he relaxed; it was coming from the wrong direction to be the Sons of Rissouli. They had driven off into the west, while this truck was approaching from the east. Moments later its headlights appeared from around a bend, travelling fast on the muddy road.

Making a snap decision, Danny stepped into the road and stuck out his thumb for a lift. To his surprise the rumbling juggernaut slid to a sudden halt in front of him. There was a brief pause before the lock popped with a clunk and the door swung slowly open. Inside, the driver, dressed in grubby jeans and a vest that might once have been white, peered down at Danny with a frown. 'Mon Dieu! Qu'est-ce que tu fais ici, toi?'

Danny decided that he was going to learn to speak French as soon as he got home. Everybody in Africa seemed to be speaking it. 'Um… Hello. Do you speak English?' he asked.

'Yes. A little. Do you need help?'

'Well, I'm a bit lost. Can you give me a lift to the nearest town?'

'A bit lost… hmm, you are saying something! What town you look for?'

'Er…I don't really know, the nearest town with a British Embassy, I suppose.'

'Hmm. Guess that will be Dakar. It is where I go now. It is... de la chance. Where you come from? ...and I don't mean Britain!' The driver laughed suddenly.

'Well, the last place I *know* I've been was near Zagora in Morocco.'

There was a long pause as the truck driver regarded Danny, his face suddenly expressionless. He appeared to be thinking, mulling over what he had heard. To Danny's surprise, there was little shock or puzzlement in the man's thin, dark face. If there was a sign of anything at all, it was sympathy.

'Hmm. Guess you better get in, boy. You're a long way from home.'

Danny clambered up into the cab and sat down heavily in the vacant seat next to the driver. Inside the darkly-lit cab an enormous array of switches and dials glowed softly. The crowning glory of this muted lightshow was a plastic Jesus, mounted centrally on top of the dashboard, arms raised in an unending blessing and lit from within by the light of God, which in this case took the form of two AA batteries and a 3 volt bulb.

There was a coughing grunt and a shudder as Danny's saviour threw the truck into gear and soon they were rumbling swiftly through the night, on their way to Dakar.

'My name,' said the driver, removing a bony hand from the steering wheel and holding it out for a handshake, '...is Omar. Yours is?'

'Danny. Danny Lansing. Pleased to meet you.' He took the proffered hand and shook, smiling inwardly at the solemnity of the greeting.

'Where are your father and mother, Danny Lansing?'

'Um… they're dead.'

Danny realised, given his current circumstances, that this statement needed some explanation. 'I live with my uncle now. We are here, um…' he looked up at Omar, wondering if he should try to tell him his story. It was a long, complicated and fanciful-sounding tale but he was too tired to make up a more plausible reason for being in Senegal. He took a deep breath and said, 'We are here investigating an international gun-running gang.'

Omar gave a slow nod of understanding, his expression giving nothing away. From his reaction, one might have believed that he gave lifts to young British lads on the trail of gangsters all the time. At last, he turned and smiled a kindly smile. 'Really?'

Danny wondered if Omar believed him, or if he was merely humouring a lost child. It didn't really matter, he was just happy to have someone friendly to talk to. 'Yes, really. I'll tell you what, if I can have any food you have going spare, I will tell you all about it.'

'That sounds a good deal, boy. These drives…' Omar indicated the endless road swooping hypnotically into the beam of the headlights and under the wheels, 'They seem to last many years. Your story will pass some time.' He smiled again, looking like a gentle prophet in the glow of his dials. 'Look in the back, there are some bananas and perhaps a little bread and, ah… thon?…no, in English it is 'tuna'.'

Danny searched behind the seats and quickly found the black

plastic bag that contained these heavenly delights. Before long he had made himself a rough tuna sandwich and had tucked a couple of bananas into his pockets for later. He began to tell the driver his story, starting with his and Angus's trip to London, their meetings with Newby and Professor Moon and their decision to travel to Morocco. He told Omar about their trip through Europe and their adventure with Mohammed and Aghilas. But as he related the drive south over the Atlas Mountains and his first sight of the Sahara, he felt his eyelids start to droop. Danny tried to stay awake but fatigue won, his eyes closed, his voice dropped to a murmur and he fell into the soundest sleep he had had for a long, long time.

★ ★ ★

Danny woke as dawn was flooding the African landscape with a fresh, golden light. The morning sun glistened on the wet leaves and drew sinuous curls of mist from the sodden ground. The road had become a broad swathe of smooth tarmac scything its way through the cultivated countryside on the outskirts of Dakar.

'Ah. You are awake.' Omar turned in his seat and smiled, but kept both hands wrapped over the steering wheel, knuckles like a row of conkers on a string. 'We are nearly there. I am not sure where your embassy is, but it will not take long. We will find it, no problem.' He grinned, a reassuring flash of white teeth and gold fillings. 'We will ask the way…'

Danny gazed out the window at the passing landscape:

a landscape bursting with the clamour of life. There were farms here, cultivated land and wandering livestock. Low buildings with deep porches and corrugated iron roofs lined the road. Some were homes, some were cafés and shops, and others were workshops that were blackened with oil and soot. And all around, engaged in the colourful hullabaloo of African life, were people: good, honest, hard-working everyday people. Not thugs and smugglers, murderers or gangsters, just ordinary folk living their lives. Danny felt suddenly and profoundly safe in a way he hadn't for a long time.

The outskirts of Dakar seemed to stretch on forever in an endless succession of rough wooden and corrugated iron buildings. Here the road was thick with traffic: a noisy, choking tumult of trucks, cars and motorbikes. Above the rumble and whine of engines came shouts, the honking of horns and the barking of stray dogs. It all came as a blessed relief after the cruel silence of the desert.

As they drove, the buildings slowly grew in stature, becoming sturdier and more permanent-looking. Concrete replaced wood and corrugated iron as the building material and a cat's cradle of overhead wires announced a proliferation of electricity and telephones. At last they reached central Dakar, weaving their way to the British Embassy.

Omar drove with his window open, shouting in French to the passersby, 'Ay! Où est l'ambassade britannique?'

But no-one knew, they shrugged their shoulders or shook their heads in apology. At last, a skinny youth in a shirt and tie gave a nod and pointed. 'C'est dans le Rue du Dr Guillet.'

Omar smiled and waved at the lad, then turned to Danny. 'It is good. I know this street. You will soon be there.'

Sure enough, a few minutes later, Omar's truck rumbled to a halt in front of the British Embassy and Danny jumped down. He turned and thanked Omar for his help, but Omar just shrugged and smiled down at him. 'It is no problem. I am coming this way anyway. Good luck Danny Lansing, I hope you find your uncle.'

He held out his hand. Danny gripped it firmly in his own and shook it. 'I'm sure I will. He always turns up in the end. Thanks again and goodbye.'

★ ★ ★

A minute or so later and Danny found himself in a spacious, air-conditioned room, facing a wide, old-fashioned desk. Behind it sat a severe-looking man whose hair had been arranged with the same astonishing symmetry as the creases in his starched shirt, which looked sharp enough to be dangerous. Under the desk, Danny could see himself reflected in the toes of a pair of highly polished shoes. Above him an enormous portrait of Queen Elizabeth II gazed down on this tiny, distant corner of the United Kingdom of Great Britain & Northern Ireland. The man's attention remained firmly fixed on a piece of paper in front of him.

'Ahem.'

The man slowly shifted his gaze to regard this intruder into his domain. 'Yes?'

'Er... I'm...' Again Danny struggled to know where to start. 'It's a long story.'

The man glanced down at his sheet of paper and sighed. 'Before you tell me it, I must ask. Are you British?'

'Yes.'

'And you are in trouble?'

'Yes.'

'Of course. As sartorially dishevelled as modern youth seems to be, you are rather more dishevelled than most.'

'Oh, yes. Sorry about that. It's been a hard few days.'

The man set his sheet of paper deliberately to one side and indicated a chair by the wall. 'Pull up a chair and tell me about it. Start at the beginning.'

And so Danny told his story again, all the time feeling scrutinised by the unblinking eyes of the embassy official. When he had finished the man nodded decisively.

'I think we ought to have Sir Charles listen to this...' He picked up the phone. 'Sir Charles?' he said. 'We have a young chap here with a very interesting story... yes... yes... if it isn't, then I am no judge of men... Very good, I'll bring him up.'

★ ★ ★

There was no air conditioning in the office of INTERPOL Dakar, but roof fans kept the atmosphere bearable as Danny inspected the book of mugshots the Senegalese police had provided. Sir Charles had accompanied him to the police station and sat discussing the case with Captain Diouf of the Office

Centrale de Répression du Trafic Illicite de Contrebande.

The British Embassy in Morocco had confirmed that Angus had not reported Danny's kidnap. However, a check with Moroccan customs had revealed that Angus had left Morocco at the border with Mauritania and, after a further check with Mauritanian customs, they knew that he had passed into Senegal at Rosso.

Danny slumped into the chair with relief at this confirmation that Angus had escaped the dunes – that he *was* still bullet-proof.

Danny assumed that Angus had somehow discovered where the Sons of Rissouli had taken him – or where they had intended taking him - and had made his pursuit. What had happened subsequently was a mystery; he appeared to have vanished. All they knew was that he hadn't contacted the Senegalese Police or the British Embassy. 'Who knows,' thought Danny, 'Perhaps he'll still show up.'

He flipped through the pages of photographs without recognising anyone. There was no sign of Khalid, and the other smugglers had all been wearing the hooded djellabas which had hidden their faces. The only other person he would recognise was the fat man, the one who'd tumbled down the sand dune with his trousers round his ankles before the world had exploded in gunfire.

Danny was just taking a second look at a photograph of a heavily bearded man with shifty eyes, when a young policeman burst into the office, snapped a salute and blurted out some remarkable news. 'Captain, gentlemen.' He nodded to Danny and Sir Charles. 'We have found a truck.'

'What truck? This blue one of the kidnappers?' asked Captain Diouf.

'No sir. We have found a red Toyota with a British registration.'

'That's Angus's!' Danny leapt up from his seat.

'On the side it says…' The policeman consulted his note-book: 'Ouch… ter… much-tee… um… plumbing co… Your sewage is our bread and butter? … yes that is right… bread and butter.'

'Yes, yes!' Danny cried, elated.

Then he remembered the mugshots. '*And* I know this guy…' He pointed to a photograph of the bearded man. 'He was with Khalid at the well. He is clean-shaven now, but that is definitely him. He's a heavyset guy… fat, I guess you would say. He probably has sand in his underpants…'

'Sand in his underpants?' asked Sir Charles.

'You had to be there to see what happened. Where did you find the Toyota?' Danny asked the young policeman.

'It is in the dockyard district in the East of Dakar, parked up a little lane. It looks like it has been in an accident.'

'What kind of accident?' Danny imagined the pick-up bullet riddled, burnt out and spattered with blood.

'Like it hit something at the front right corner. It has been repaired, but poorly.'

Danny wondered what this meant but took heart in the knowledge that surely no-one else would bother to repair such a vehicle. Still, it was difficult to say how finding the abandoned vehicle would help them find Angus.

At this point Captain Diouf spoke up. 'You say you recognise this man in the photo?'

'Yes, I'm sure this man was at the well in Algeria where we saw the guns being smuggled. He looks older now and has lost the beard.'

Captain Diouf picked up the book and examined the picture. For a moment he remained silent, his brow furrowed with concentration. 'Hmm. I know this man from somewhere. The mugshot says his name is Ibrahima Lo... Wait, I have it! I arrested him myself many years ago for possession of cannabis, nothing more than a misdemeanour, really. So! He has graduated to trafficking guns? This will go badly for him.'

'I don't suppose he lives near where Angus's pick-up was found?' asked Danny.

'It's unlikely. Dakar docks is an area of industrialisation – workshops and warehouses. Nobody lives there. If Lo has a connection to the area, it is more likely because he works there.'

Captain Diouf rubbed his hands together and smiled at Danny.

'I will have my men look into Mr Lo and see what they can find. Do not worry, we have several leads to follow. We will find your uncle and, who knows, we may break an arms smuggling operation while we are at it!'

CHAPTER EIGHT

Angus woke suddenly, a rush of nausea causing his eyes to snap open. Cold sweat beaded on his forehead and the room span. The moment of dizziness soon passed, however, and consciousness returned in all its painful, throbbing reality. It was many years since he'd felt this bad and he dimly remembered that the last time had involved falling out of a helicopter.

He was still tied to the chair in the office, but now a pale luminosity filtering through the window suggested that it was no longer the middle of the night. A faintly golden quality to the light implied it was either just after dawn or early evening. He wondered what would happen next.

He did not have to wait long to find out. A few minutes later the door opened and in walked the black shirted thug. He was carrying a tray on which were two tall glasses of mint tea.

'Good Evening,' he said, pulling the chair from behind his desk and sitting down. His manner was much more relaxed than it had been the previous night. He even smiled.

'I'm afraid we got off to a bad start.' Another smile, like a crocodile with wind. 'You must understand, I am a business man. I have responsibilities - employees, families to feed. I cannot afford to have someone threaten that. That is not unreasonable, I think?'

'No.'

'Good. I am glad you understand. My name is Khalid. Perhaps you will tell me yours?'

'Angus.'

Angus knew what was going on, it was an interrogation technique he'd heard about before. Heaven and Hell. You start with Hell – you beat your prisoner up, torture them, starve them, fill their lives with pain and suffering. Then you switch. Like Jekyll and Hyde. You become friendly, reasonable and kind. You offer food, drink and a respite from the pain of torture. It feels like Heaven in comparison. The person being interrogated becomes desperate to stay in Heaven and starts to talk, knowing that when they stop they are going straight back to Hell. If it doesn't work the first time, you repeat the cycle until it does.

Everyone cracks eventually.

'Would you like some tea?'

Angus nearly laughed.

'Yes please.'

Khalid picked up one of the glasses and tipped it towards Angus's lips. It tasted wonderful. The hot liquid soothed his parched tongue and lips and he immediately felt much better. This was certainly preferable to being punched in the face.

Angus realised that this was a very tricky situation. If he simply explained that he was a journalist investigating gun-running, Khalid would have all the information he needed and would murder him. No, he would have to tease the thug with information in order to prolong their conversation…

and his life.

'So, you work for Brunton?'

'Yes.' Angus knew the lie was his only hope of staying alive.

Khalid shifted in his chair and stared for a moment through the window of the office.

'I suspected. I have never trusted Brunton. There is something...' he searched for the word, '...condescending, about him. As though we Amazigh are below him.'

'You've met him then?'

'Of course. There is only so much business you can do over the phone.' He smiled his crocodilian smile again and leaned forward. 'So. What was the plan? How did you intend to rip me off?'

Angus thought furiously. He'd have to come up with a convincing story right now, or he'd be killed. The secret in a successful lie, he knew, was to stay vague, stick with what you know and to try to include a few truths to give it some authenticity.

'There is no plan.'

'No plan?!' Khalid looked unconvinced and irritated. Angus spoke up quickly.

'Yes. There's no real *plan*. He hasn't got that far yet. And he isn't – wasn't - going to just rip you off. He was going to take over your whole operation.'

'WHAT!?' Khalid jumped up, his face twisted with rage. Angus saw his hands curl into fists and realised he had gone too far. He braced himself for the inevitable punch... but it didn't come. With an effort, the gangster controlled himself. He sat back in his chair, shaking.

'My whole operation? How could he do that? You do not simply turn up in Africa and take over the business of Khalid Rissouli! Ha ha!' He was smiling again, as though amused by Brunton's cheek, but beneath the smile Angus could see intense anger.

'Like I said, there was no plan as yet. I was simply to come down here and see how everything worked, see if there were any weaknesses that could be exploited. Like the paperwork – the end user certificates and such. Your man on the inside... um...' Angus closed his eyes as though trying to remember a name.

'Ibrahima Lo?' said Khalid. 'Yes, he is certainly a weakness. The man is stupid and cowardly. Unfortunately we need his military connections to get the certificates. Without him... But anyway, I do not understand why Brunton would want to change our arrangement. It is very profitable for both of us.'

Time for a little truth to add authenticity, thought Angus.

'Why do you think he grinds the serial numbers off the weapons before he sends them to you?'

Khalid glared. 'You tell me.'

'Because he doesn't trust you to do the job properly yourselves.'

Khalid snorted, as though the suggestion was ridiculous.

'Brunton is paranoid that you'll screw up. He thinks the only way to be sure that you don't is to run everything himself.'

Angus stared hard into Khalid's face. 'He thinks you are stupid enough to leave some hard evidence somewhere that links him directly to you. Evidence that could put him in jail.'

Khalid's eyes twitched to the left. It was a barely perceptible flicker but Angus saw it. The gangster had glanced straight at the filing cabinet.

Khalid was staring at him now. A silent, baleful stare. There was no longer any suggestion of friendliness. The pretence was over. There would be no more mint tea and smiles.

'So he thinks I am stupid? We'll see about that! I will deal with Lord Brunton myself.'

He stood and thrust his leather chair back behind his desk.

'But first you. You have proved yourself extremely dangerous.'

He reached behind his back and pulled a handgun from the waistband of his trousers.

'Wait!' Angus frantically tried to think of something to say that would buy him more time.

Khalid shrugged and lifted his gun.

'For what? You have told me everything I need to know!"

'Not everything...'

BANG! BANG! BANG! BANG!

The noise of an automatic rifle hammered through the warehouse, followed by panicked shouts from near the door. Seconds later there was more gunfire, this time from outside. Khalid's eyes opened wide and he leapt to the office window to see what was happening. Then he turned back towards Angus, lifted his gun, pulled back the slide and smiled.

★ ★ ★

'Messieurs!'

Captain Diouf reached up and rapped his knuckles on the van's roof to get the attention of the twelve policemen who made up the raiding team. He cast a swift glance down at his watch and began. 'Dans cinq minutes...'

He spoke quickly and authoritatively, occasionally indicating one of the policemen with a pointed finger. The policemen were tough young men in black combat clothing, carrying M16 assault rifles. They sat in stony-faced concentration, absorbing every word spoken. The only flicker of movement from them was the occasional tiny nod of assent to an order given by the Captain. Danny could not follow exactly what was being said, but understood the gist of it.

★ ★ ★

Things had moved pretty fast after Danny recognised the face of the fat smuggler amongst the mugshots. Captain Diouf had discovered that Ibrahima Lo had, until a year ago, been a clerk in the Senegalese Army. Now it seemed he was working for the Compagnie Dakar Expedition shipping business. Danny had laughed at this and told Captain Diouf how it was the name of the shipping company whose details Angus had retrieved from the house in Chefchaouen.

A check into the company's interests had revealed that it

owned a warehouse in East Dakar, just a couple of hundred yards from where the Toyota had been found. It had been decided, based on Danny's evidence and Ibrahima Lo's criminal record, to mount a raid on the warehouse. If, as seemed likely, Angus had investigated the warehouse earlier and fallen foul of the Sons of Rissouli, the sooner they raided it the better. The time was set for 7.30 pm the following day.

Newby, following a phone call from Sir Charles, had arrived the next day at 3 in the afternoon, on the Air France flight from London, Heathrow. He breezed into the INTERPOL Dakar office like it was his home from home, greeted Captain Diouf with a hearty handshake and asked for 'the low-down'. Captain Diouf had simply nodded and passed over a folder containing all the information they had on the case.

'The team is arranged to raid the warehouse this evening,' Captain Diouf told Newby once he had finished reading.

'Good. I'd like to be in the team. Just as an observer, of course,' Newby said in an offhand manner, as though the request was obvious and Captain Diouf's agreement a formality.

Danny got the feeling Diouf had been ambushed by the request before he had had time to think it over. 'Of course,' replied the officer.

'Good,' said Newby. Then, quickly changing the subject, he added, 'Before we go any further, however, I'm starving. The meal on my flight wouldn't have fed a hamster. Do you chaps have a cafeteria?'

★ ★ ★

And so, a few hours later, Danny found himself sitting in the back of a large blue police van with Captain Diouf, Newby, twelve heavily-armed policemen and a paramedic. Captain Diouf finished briefing his men and turned to Newby.

'Chief Inspector, you should follow me in, I think. You are not carrying a weapon, so it would be best if you stay well back. If the evidence is correct, we are dealing with some very well-armed criminals.'

'Fine.'

'Danny, I'm afraid you must stay here with the medic. You are a little young for this type of thing.'

'I understand.' Danny knew the raid would be dangerous, but he could not help feeling a little disappointed that he would have to remain behind in the van.

Captain Diouf moved to the rear of the van and pushed open its doors. The sky outside was the deepest turquoise and scattered with high clouds lit with the orange fire of the African evening. As the policemen streamed out, they disappeared quickly into the dark shadows thrown by the setting sun. Danny suddenly understood the logic behind choosing this time for the raid. The policemen were approaching the warehouse from the west, with the sunset directly behind them. When they weren't concealed in deep shadow, the glare of the sun on the horizon would make them equally difficult to spot.

★ ★ ★

Newby stifled a smile as he moved in a crouching run behind

Captain Diouf, towards the Sons of Rissouli's warehouse. There had been a time, many years ago, when this kind of thing had been his *raison d'etre*. It was why, as a lad, he had joined the Guards and then had himself seconded to a less 'regular' branch of the army. It was why he had had a brief flirtation with the Secret Intelligence Service (until he realised his principles were a little too 'black and white' for the murky-grey world of espionage) and why, after twenty years in the police, he still spent as little of his time as possible behind his desk in New Scotland Yard.

He found the old crouching-run thing a little less comfortable than he used to and his gammy knee had stiffened up in the last few years, making him a shade less agile, but the peculiar mixture of apprehension and exhilaration was the same as it had always been. He had to admit it; while he was primarily here to help Angus because he felt responsible for getting him involved with the Sons of Rissouli, he was also here because there promised to be a generous slice of excitement.

They approached in short, sudden sprints. Moving from shadow to shadow, always watching the warehouse for movement. Newby caught glimpses of policemen passing down nearby lanes as they spread out to encircle the building. He was pleased with the team; it was disciplined and efficient and its members worked well together. Whatever happened next, it was vital that these men kept their heads.

They were close now; barely fifty yards away. There was no sign of life on the hot, deserted streets. It was as though the locals had sensed that something dangerous was going to happen and had made themselves scarce. Even the rats normally seen scurrying amongst the trash and along the gutters had gone to ground. Newby wondered if the Sons of Rissouli also knew they were coming.

A final dash took them over the last stretch of open ground to the gates. A tall, square-shouldered policeman appeared with a pair of long-handled bolt cutters. With a metallic snap, the padlock fell useless to the ground. Newby watched the policemen slip down the side streets and position themselves in strategic locations; two on the roofs of nearby buildings, one behind a pile of pallets and another behind an abandoned car. The other eight were now following Captain Diouf through the open gates and making for the front doors.

And it was all going to plan until that moment.

The smallest of the doors burst open. All that could be seen inside was darkness. The raiding party dropped to their knees and shouldered their weapons. Newby glanced at Captain Diouf as he opened his mouth to issue an order, but it was too late. From the open doorway came a flash and the reverberating banging of an assault rifle being fired.

Newby hit the ground and rolled as gunfire exploded from the warehouse. Bullets flew through the air with a low pitched whizz, hitting concrete with a 'PAFF!' and metal with a 'WHANG!' A second later the rapid 'CRACK, CRACK, CRACK!' of the police M16s echoed across the forecourt; an area that now seemed enormous.

Then Newby heard a sound that filled him with horror: the unmistakeable and unforgettable wet thump of bullets tearing into a human body. He turned to see the tall policeman with the bolt cutters stagger, fall and writhe on the ground, clawing at his chest and swearing. Swearing to stop himself from screaming.

Without a weapon Newby could not return fire. He jumped up and scrambled over to the stricken man, feeling suddenly and hideously vulnerable in the gunfire that fizzed about him like a swarm of angry wasps. Grabbing an arm he pulled the man to his feet, ignoring the stream of abuse which the wounded policeman now directed at him.

'Shut up and cover the wound with your hand!' Newby shouted, dragging him towards a dumpster parked just outside the warehouse gates. It was barely twenty-five metres away and yet it seemed impossibly distant. They were moving painfully slowly and he expected to feel the tearing heat of a bullet in his back with every crack and whine that rent the evening air. The policeman was heavy, damned heavy, and Newby's legs felt weak with the effort of supporting him. He could smell him too, smell the sweat of fear which soaked the man's uniform. He was spitting blood now, bright red froth bubbling on his lips. Slowly, so slowly, they made their way towards cover.

A long burst of gunfire clattered out behind and there was another sickening wet thump. The policeman shuddered and went suddenly limp.

'Jesus… C'mon you great lump! I'm too damn old to carry you…'

The policeman had been hit again, in the thigh this time.

The stream of profanities stopped, replaced by a low moaning. Newby's knees buckled as the full weight of the dying man fell on his shoulders. Only a couple of metres to go, he could not give up now. Newby drew a deep breath and dragged once more. Another member of the raiding party passed in a staggering run, carrying a wounded comrade in a fireman's lift. Things were not going well.

'Battez en RETRAITE!' The shout came from Captain Diouf. He had clearly decided discretion was the better part of valour. At last, in a final massive effort, Newby pulled the policeman behind the dumpster. Looking up at it he realised it was only a square box of thin steel filled with rubbish; a bullet from a military rifle would pass straight through it, but it was better than nothing. At least the murderous thugs would no longer be able to see them.

Captain Diouf joined them a few seconds later, his jaw clenched tight and his eyes dark with anger. Looking to the snipers on the rooftops, he pressed the 'transmit' button on his radio and yelled a series of instructions. He then turned to Newby, who was tying a bootlace round the man's injured leg in a rudimentary tourniquet.

'How bad is he?'

'Bad. The leg's serious enough, a bullet has nicked his artery, but his real problem is the sucking chest wound. If we don't do something now he will be dead in minutes. Do you have a First Aid kit in those pouches?'

'Yes, but it is pretty basic. We have the paramedic for serious injuries.'

'Your man could be dead by the time he gets here. Does your kit contain medical tape or a dressing?'

Three shots thudded violently into the dumpster. Newby and Captain Diouf ducked, but the bullets did not pass through. Perhaps the dumpster was tougher than Newby had thought. A clatter of return fire poured down from the rooftop snipers and from the raiding team who were now spread out behind any available cover. The Sons of Rissouli were silenced, at least for the moment.

'It's hotter than Hades behind this ruddy trash can!'

Captain Diouf laughed weakly, the comment lost on him.

Then he remembered Newby's request. 'I have dressings, yes… and I have this…' He handed two rolls to Newby. 'Will these do?'

'Duct tape will do the job, but the ordinary dressing is no good. We need something that will make an airtight seal over the wound and stop his lungs collapsing. Do you have a polythene bag?'

'No. I'm sorry.'

'It's all right, I may have something.' Newby rummaged in his trouser pocket and pulled out the contents: a bag of Jelly Babies. 'I *knew* these would come in handy!' He ripped open the bag, spilling the multi-coloured sweets over the ground. Using his pocket knife he cut a piece out of the plastic wrapping about ten centimetres square. Meanwhile, the wounded man's breathing had dropped to shallow, rapid gasps and he had slipped into complete unconsciousness.

Ripping open the man's shirt, Newby wiped away the excess

blood. Carefully placing the square of yellow plastic over the wound, he stuck it down using pieces of Captain Diouf's duct tape. Almost immediately the man's breathing became slower and deeper. Newby then rolled him onto his side, so that his wounded lung was closest to the ground, hoping it would stop the man's good lung from filling with blood.

'Right, that seems to have sorted him out for the moment,' said Newby. 'Now, I'd get on to that medic of yours. He needs proper treatment as soon as possible.'

'Of course.' Captain Diouf got back on his radio.

Another burst of gunfire hammered out of the warehouse door in the direction of the dumpster. Two bullets thudded into it and more ripped into the ground nearby. An answering salvo streamed into the warehouse from the police M16s, the policemen's bullets tearing long lines of ragged holes in its metal walls.

Suddenly a loud explosion boomed inside. A cloud of smoke rolled from the open doorway and a man began to scream.

'What on earth was that?' asked Captain Diouf.

'Sounded like a grenade...or a rocket from a hand-held launcher. Not sure why they would set it off inside their own warehouse though. Maybe it was an accident, or perhaps one of our bullets hit something?'

Four more explosions, exactly like the first, rang out in quick succession. The screaming stopped. More smoke poured from the doorway, thicker and darker this time. Soon, it was seeping in thin, curling fingers from skylights in the building's roof.

'Good God!' cried Newby. 'I think the warehouse

has caught fire!'

A series of smaller reports echoed inside the smoking hulk, like a string of firecrackers going off. Muffled shouts rang out, followed by more explosions. For a few seconds a cacophony of bangs and thuds echoed from within the warehouse. There were more panicked yells and another scream. Through the darkened doorway Newby could see the flash of explosions tearing the place apart. Nothing, he thought, could survive in there, in that enclosed space filled with flying shards of burning-hot metal.

★ ★ ★

'Oui, Capitaine.' The medic spat out his gum and shouldered his medical pack. Without a word to Danny, he opened the rear door of the van, jumped down and ran off in the direction of the warehouse. Danny was left alone, to stare after him down the deserted street.

He had listened excitedly, but also anxiously, to the sounds of the gun-battle. Some would think a raid was thrilling stuff, but Danny was too concerned about Angus to feel it. If Angus was being held in the warehouse he would almost certainly get caught up in the fighting. If he was tied up or handcuffed he would not be able to defend himself or take cover from the flying bullets. Danny tried to dismiss these thoughts. After all, wasn't Angus bullet-proof...?

His anxiety turned to horror as the noise of the fighting got louder, escalating in violence and ferocity. He had expected the gun-battle to be a short-lived affair. The team of policemen had seemed such a formidable force that he had not imagined the criminals would hold out for long against them.

But when Captain Diouf came on the radio calling for the medic, Danny knew things were not going to plan. And now, just moments after the medic had raced out to help, came the dull, flat boom of an explosion. It was rapidly followed by four more, before the vicious crackle of gunfire resumed. Danny could not see the warehouse from where he was, but he knew it was only a few hundred yards away, hidden behind the ramshackle ruins of a disused sawmill.

As he stared in the direction of the noise, he became aware of a grey haze hanging above the rooftops. It rapidly thickened into a dark column, a dense pall of billowing smoke, rising straight into the still evening air. Danny realised what was happening at once: the warehouse was on fire! He felt a prickle of panic. What if Angus was inside? What if he was trapped, or locked in a room?

He hesitated, his mind racing. He had been told to stay where he was. If he got out of the van and headed for the gun-battle he would not only be *risking* his life; he would get the most spectacular bollocking of it. If he made it back alive he would consider himself lucky if he was allowed to see a TV again before he was eighteen. However, deep down he knew that if there ever had been a time to do what he was told, it was now. But then he thought of Angus.

'Sod it.'

Kicking open the van door, he jumped out and charged

towards the smoke. As he got closer, the sound of gunfire intensified. It was as though a hundred machine-guns were emptying their magazines at once. Another, louder, series of explosions made him start. The vibrations shuddered through the earth as he ran. It sounded like a full-scale war was taking place around the corner.

As he passed the sawmill on his right and the warehouse came into view, Danny's mouth fell open at a sight like nothing he had ever imagined. Thick black smoke and rippling heat blurred the details, making it seem unreal, like a movie. The entire building was ablaze, showering sparks and cinders onto a scene of intense destruction. There were bullet holes in everything; lines of ragged punctures that criss-crossed every surface. The blood-covered ground was scattered with fragments of glass, timber and metal, the debris of a dozen explosions and cartridge cases from countless rounds of ammunition. Danny stopped running and stood transfixed, trying to think what he should do.

'DANNY!'

The shout snapped him out of his momentary daze.

'What in God's name are you doing? Get over here, you fool!'

It was Newby, beckoning to him from behind a dumpster. With him was Captain Diouf, who was glaring disbelievingly in Danny's direction. Oh, he was in trouble all right.

Between them, the paramedic was attending to a blood-soaked policeman. The policeman was not moving. The banging of exploding cartridges reminded him of the vulnerability of his position and he sprinted for the cover of the dumpster.

'What the…' began Newby, before Danny interrupted.

'Where's Angus? Is he in the warehouse?'

'We don't know. What the hell are you doing here? You were told to stay in the van!'

'I needed to find out what was happening.' Danny risked a quick glance round the dumpster at the burning warehouse. 'My uncle could be in there! He could be burning to death right now and we're just sitting here!'

'We don't know that and we can't get close enough to find out. All those bangs you can hear? That's bullets exploding as they catch fire… and possibly grenades too. It would be absolute lunacy to go in there right now. To be honest, Danny, our only hope is that Angus is being held somewhere else, because the chances of anyone surviving in there are a thousand to one.'

Thick, black smoke was belching through the doorway and from where explosions had torn holes in the roof. A constant staccato of exploding bullets confirmed Newby's opinion of how dangerous it would be to try to get inside. Danny felt suddenly sick, the awful, numbing sickness of personal loss. It was dreadfully familiar. He had felt this way when he had lost his parents and now it seemed likely he had lost Angus too, because he was certain his uncle was still inside, either dying slowly or already dead. And there was nothing he could do.

What if Danny was trapped in a burning building with bullets and grenades exploding all around him? What would Angus do? Danny knew the answer to that. Taking a deep breath, he grinned nervously at Newby. Then he jumped up and sprinted furiously for the smoking doorway of the burning warehouse.

'DANNY! Get back here! You stupid son of a… Oh, for crying out loud!'

Danny heard the shout, but ignored it. All his attention was focused on that blackened doorway. A second shout rang out.

'Chief Inspector! Danny! Ah… Mon Dieu, l'anglais stupide!'

Turning briefly to see what was happening, Danny saw Newby pounding after him across the concrete and, just a few steps behind, Captain Diouf. He wondered if they were trying to catch him and pull him back, or if they were coming to help him find Angus. Whichever it was, he wasn't going to hang around to find out.

He could feel the heat of the fire as he got close. It was tangible, a sudden wall of blisteringly hot air that almost stopped him in his tracks. Coming from inside he could hear bullets exploding and the roar of the flames as they consumed the building and all of its contents. He plunged into the murk, covering his mouth with his hand in a futile effort to keep the smoke from his lungs. Around him he could see the dim outlines of shelving disappearing into blackness. To his right, the end of the warehouse was an inferno of red flames. Yellow flashes of exploding ordnance flared briefly amongst the blaze, while the whizzing of flying lead carried with it the threat of sudden death or terrible injury.

'ANGUS!' He paused to listen for an answer. None came.

'ANGUS!' Still nothing.

Newby and Captain Diouf appeared at this moment,

staggering blindly through the smoke. Newby glanced at the nearest crates.

'Danny, we have to get out of here! This place is crammed to the gills with high explosive, it's going to go up at any moment!'

'I can't give up! I have to see if Angus is in here!' Danny turned away and shouted again into the smoke and flames. 'ANGUS!'

Perhaps they were too late to save him. Perhaps he had already succumbed to the fumes, or been killed by a stray bullet or flying shrapnel. Danny was choking now and feeling faint, his eyes streaming with tears as the fumes stung at his eyes.

'Come on, boy!' demanded Newby, pulling Danny towards the door.

And then Danny heard a shout. It was muffled, indistinct and weak. But it was a shout of his name and he recognised the voice instantly.

'ANGUS?' Newby and Danny shouted simultaneously.

'In here! In the office!'

Danny, Newby and Captain Diouf ran towards the office, through scattered pieces of twisted metal that were strewn across the floor. Its fibre-board walls had been punctured by shrapnel and its window lay in fragments amongst the debris, but it had provided just enough protection to save Angus's life so far. The door was locked.

'Stand aside!' said Newby, giving the door a hefty kick close to the handle. The whole office shook with the blow as the door splintered and cracked, but did not give way. Newby rocked back on his heels and then heaved his shoulder into it.

A groan, a bang, and the door disintegrated.

The three of them jumped in at once. Angus had been tied to a chair, but had managed to tip himself onto the floor behind a heavy wooden desk to shield himself from flying shrapnel. Covered in blood, soot and grime, and looking like he had gone twelve rounds with the Incredible Hulk, he was nevertheless grinning widely at his rescuers.

'How's it going fellas? What say you cut me free and we get the hell out of here?'

'Sounds like a good idea! Anyone got a knife?' said Danny, a sudden wave of happiness surging through him, despite the danger. His impossible uncle was somehow all right. Angus *was* damn well bullet-proof!

Captain Diouf pulled out his pocket knife and cut Angus free. Newby helped him to his feet.

'Good God, man! You *are* in a state. The sooner we get you looked at by the pretty nurses at Dakar Hospital the better. Now, let's get out of here!'

'First things first!' Angus yanked open the drawers of the filing cabinet, pulling out the contents and thrusting them at Newby.

'Take these!' he yelled, piling file upon file into Newby's arms.

'Mr McKinlay, we MUST leave NOW!' Captain Diouf shouted above the noise of the roaring flames and exploding bullets.

Angus tore open the final drawer and pulled out the contents.

'Somewhere in here is the evidence we need to nail Brunton!' Angus grabbed one last file and cried, 'Right! Let's go!'

As they stepped to the door the air felt as if it was sucked out of the building in a single drawn breath, taking most of the flames with it. There was a brief, expectant silence. Then… BOOM!

The walls of the office bent inwards with the blast and what was left of the door was blown from its hinges. Smoke, dust and shrapnel flew in through the doorway and the shattered window. Danny felt the blast punch the air from his lungs. He was knocked off his feet and thrown to the ground. For a few seconds, everything went black and he could hear nothing but a loud ringing in his ears.

Slowly, he became aware of a voice calling his name. A hand grabbed his collar in the darkness.

'Danny! Come on mate, let's get out of this.' It was Angus. He felt himself being lifted, dragged forwards. Pushed through the choking darkness. He saw a vague rectangle of light and was propelled towards it by unseen hands. Suddenly he was outside, in the yard in front of the warehouse. Running. Running for his life.

'GO! KEEP GOING! THE WHOLE PLACE COULD GO AT ANY MINUTE!'

He turned. Behind him ran Angus, Newby and Captain Diouf. Newby had blood on his face, but was still clutching the untidy bundle of files Angus had taken from the filing cabinet.

'KEEP RUNNING!'

They ran hard across the forecourt, hearts in mouths, sucking deep breaths into aching lungs. They were through the gate. Cover! The dumpster! For the second time that day Danny dived behind a rubbish bin in fear of his life. Seconds later the others joined him.

CRACK… BANG!

A huge explosion ripped through the warehouse. The whole southern end seemed to inflate, like a balloon, then burst. Burning fragments were thrown outwards in all directions. From tiny rivets to great, ragged sheets of steel, the lethal missiles whirred, whistled and moaned through the air. They rattled off the ground, crashed into the dumpster and rained down from above. Moments later, a series of secondary explosions thudded and banged. For nearly a minute the ground shook with tremors as shrapnel flew and bright flashes lit the billowing column of smoke that rose from the shattered ruins into the evening sky.

When, at last, silence fell, it came like a blanket that smothered everything. It seemed like a force in itself, sucking the slightest whisper of sound from the surrounding streets. It demanded quiet over the funeral pyre of the Sons of Rissouli.

CHAPTER NINE

ONE WEEK LATER

Danny pulled his hands inside his sleeves in an effort to keep them dry. It was raining in the English manner, a fine drizzle pattering on his hood and running in mercurial streams down his waterproof jacket. But that was fitting, as they were in England. In Herefordshire, to be precise, at the end of the leafy driveway that led to a Victorian mansion. He was tagging along on another police raid, under strict instructions not to interfere this time. He was keeping a low profile and he found that as long as he hung back, stayed in Angus's shadow, nobody seemed to notice he was there.

Angus had been right about those files. They contained a policeman's dream - invoices, orders, accounts and those extremely revealing packing labels. Everything that was needed to draw a complete picture of the Sons of Rissouli's gun-running operation. And, tucked away amongst it all, was evidence of regular, very large, money transfers in to a Threadneedle Private Bank account held in the name of Richard Lombard. It was the same bank of which Lord Thomas Brunton was a director. Further investigation revealed that Richard Lombard did not exist. Newby needed no more evidence. A warrant was obtained, and here they were; standing in the rain in Herefordshire, waiting to raid Brunton's house.

'Ahem!' Newby cleared his throat noisily and fingered the sticking plaster on his forehead (a souvenir from the pretty nurses at Dakar Hospital). 'Ladies and Gentlemen. You all know your roles. Lord Thomas Brunton is an influential man, so I would call for a minimum of manhandling and name-calling. He is, after all, innocent until proven guilty and all that rot. However, as beautifully tailored as the ermine robes of his exalted friends may be, he is still a common criminal. Let's go in hard and fast. We do not wish to allow him time to burn, shred or flush any vital evidence. This…' he gestured in Angus's direction, 'is Angus McKinlay. He has been given special dispensation - as the journalist who brought this criminal conspiracy to our attention - to follow us in and cover the proceedings for his article. Try not to arrest him in a misplaced fit of enthusiasm.' He paused, as though he was wondering if he might have forgotten something, then said, 'Right. Let's go!'

Turning, he strode off up the driveway, leading his police officers towards the imposing black door of the Brunton residence. As Angus and Danny crunched up the gravel behind them, Danny speculated as to what Lord Brunton's reaction would be. Would he pretend to be innocent? Throw up his hands and say 'Who, me?' Or would he come clean and admit his guilt? He wondered what the upper-class equivalent of 'It's a fair cop, guv'nor!' was. As they reached the door, Newby stepped forwards and knocked loudly.

'Lord Brunton! Special Branch. Open the door!'

They paused, standing in silence for a few breathless moments. Newby tried the door and found it locked.

'Very well. Do your stuff, Martin.'

A thickset copper carrying a short battering ram stepped forward and, with a single swing, smashed the heavy door into the marble-floored hallway. The raiding team charged in, swiftly followed by Angus and Danny. In these final moments of their adventure, they were determined not to miss out on the action.

The thunder of heavy boots echoed around the cavernous old house as the Special Branch officers searched for evidence. But of Lord Thomas Brunton, there was no sign. Then, amongst the noise of banging doors and running feet, came a sudden shout from an upstairs room.

'Sir!' Then a pause… 'SIR!'

The voice was cracked with shock and uncertainty. As if the speaker could not believe his eyes.

'What is it?' called Newby. He was already halfway up the stairs, suspecting that something important had been found. Angus and Danny ran after him.

They burst into the room; a study with dark wood panelling and oil paintings on the walls. A vast oak desk sat over by the curtained window, its chair pushed hard against the wall. Danny saw no detail of the room, however, only what lay on the floor in front of him.

'It appears Lord Thomas Brunton,' said Newby, 'has had his chips.'

The respectable entrepreneur, the man of influence, the friend of the great and the good, a Peer of the Realm no less… the gun-runner, lay dead in a dark stain on his Persian rug. But

Danny's eyes were fixed on the corpse's chest, or rather, what was sticking out of it.

'The dagger!'

He pointed. 'Look at it! Look at the shape of the handle! Look at the silverwork on the pommel and the cedar-wood grip! It's exactly like the one in the body pulled from the Thames and it's the same as the ones the smugglers all carried.'

'What?' cried Newby. 'But that would mean...'

'That the Sons of Rissouli murdered him.' finished Angus.

'They must have thought he had double-crossed them!' said Danny. He looked around. Everyone was looking at him, but no-one was telling him to shut up. He stiffened as the realisation hit him. A cold shiver crept up his spine and the colour drained from his face as he whispered two words he knew to be true: 'Khalid escaped!'

They were all staring at him; Newby, Angus, the policeman who'd found Brunton's body and Martin of the battering ram. At last, Martin spoke up.

'Who the hell are you?'

Danny opened his mouth to answer, but the words did not come. A sudden wave of embarrassment overcame him and he looked at his feet. He should not be there, he knew it, he had been told not to interfere. Yet here he was, mouthing off with his theories…

'Who is this?' Angus stepped forward, coming to his rescue. 'This is Danny Lansing – investigative journalist!'

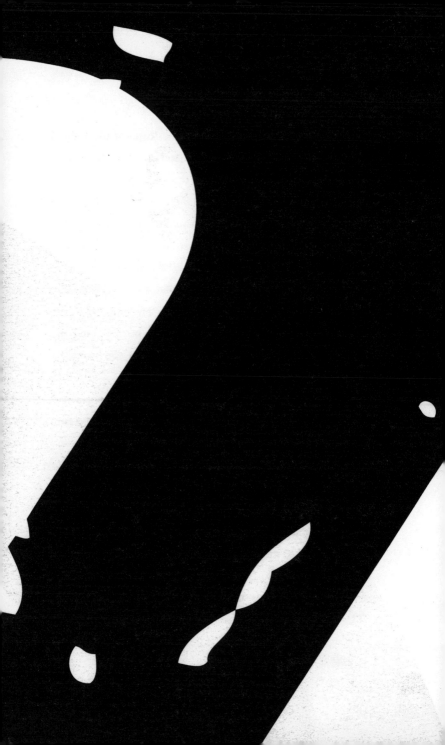

The end?

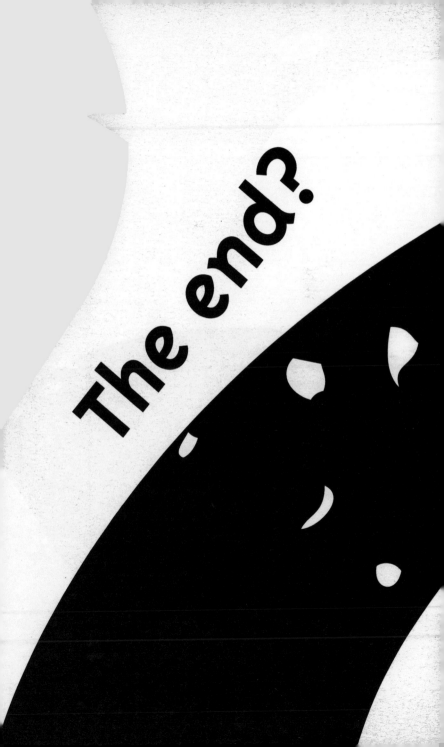

ACKNOWLEDGEMENTS

Firstly, I'd like to thank my mum and dad. My mum for ensuring I grew up with a love of reading and my dad for providing a vast and varied library of adventure stories. I'd also like to thank my mum for her initial proof reading of 'The Sons of Rissouli'. Her corrections undoubtedly helped the book get published!

Many thanks also to everyone at Strident Publishing – Keith Charters and Alison Stroak for their expert help and advice with the promotion of the book, to Graham Watson for his skilled and sympathetic editing, Lawrence Mann for his superb cover and interior graphics and to Marion Bourbouze and Damien Love for correcting my schoolboy French!

–Matt Cartney

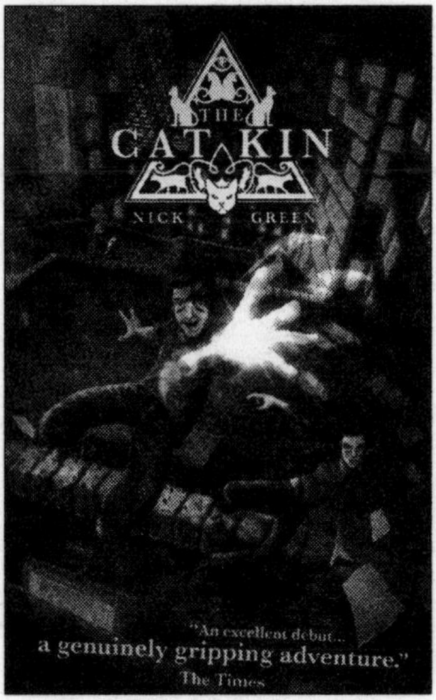

The Cat Kin

ISBN 978-1-905537-16-7 (paperback, RRP £6.99)

Everyone who came to the strange gym class was looking for something else. What they found was the mysterious Mrs Powell and Pashki, a lost art from an age when cats were worshipped as gods.

Ben and Tiffany wonder: who is their eccentric old teacher? What does she really want with them? And why are they suddenly able to see in the dark?

Meanwhile, in London's gloomy streets, human vermin are stirring. Ben and Tiffany may soon be glad of their new gifts. But against men whose cunning is matched only by their unspeakable cruelty, will even nine lives be enough?

Spider

ISBN 978-1-905537-06-8 (paperback, RRP £6.99)

A hard-hitting and provocative novel about teenage love, loyalty and fast cars.

Spider is on his last warning. If he's caught joyriding again he'll be sent down, no questions asked. He's trying to stick to the straight and narrow but his girlfriend Deanna and mate Andy reckon he should risk one last run.

Spider is an adrenaline-fuelled ride — a compelling glimpse into a life spinning out of control.

Lee and the Consul Mutants

ISBN 978-1-905537-24-2 (paperback, RRP £6.99)

It's not every day that a part of your body explodes, but Lee's appendix does exactly that, landing him in hospital.

Soon after his operation, Lee is shocked to discover that evil Consul Mutants are trying to take over the world. Worse still, the hospital he is stuck in contains the portal they are using to invade Earth.

Other kids might quake in their boots at this news, but not Lee. He's determined to save the world and comes up with a cunning plan to stop the aliens.

This is the story of a young boy battling against intergalactic odds for the sake of humankind. Lee's only weapon is his intelligence… which is a pity.